DIAMOND SPIRES

DIAMOND SPIRES

A NOVEL

BY PETER BJORNDAL

FRIENDLY PUPPY PRESS

2019

DIAMOND SPIRES

BOOK I

CHAPTER ONE

"Do you wanna do anything?"

"A little bit. I think I could do something."

"You wanna go walk around maybe?"

"That sounds potentially fruitful."

"Alright, let's head outta here."

The two stepped out the door onto the road and started walking. Nuru spoke again: "I wanna hit up the FDC and sorta want to go past the floaty things even though we did that yesterday." He buttoned up his outer layer. "There's an element to them I find uncanny yet soothing which creates an effect of some word that means uncanny and soothing."

"Yeah, we can do that."

Nuru was wearing taut tan pants and a tan jacket most assumed chino cloth, but was bleached and re-dyed denim. After a few steps, the fabric started rubbing against his thighs and he made a quick adjustment. Even though he was monochromatic, he liked his tan chic which he thought complemented his skin tone. Walking in sync with Gwendoline was a bigger confidence booster, though.

"You know what's funny?" she said, not waiting for a reply. "I've had this thought in my head for the past couple of days. I'm starting to think that my taste in Victorian and baroque furniture is rooted in some sort of primal sense of reactionary elitism." She frowned and unfocused her eyes at the ground.

Nuru squinted at a cloud and frowned slightly. "There's a lot to unpack there." To anyone but her, his voice was perfectly earnest, but Gwendoline picked up his mockery. She ignored it and jerked up her head to look down the road.

"Well, it was the furniture of the high class in the era of Queen Victoria or whatever—I'm assuming at least. Now today we can look back and see that, yes, it is still beautiful, but there are other styles of furniture that look just as good, and perhaps better. Why do *I* like it? Is it because I think it looks good, or is it because I associate it with a period in history where a brutally rigid social structure was romanticized with kings and queens and knights and people eating whole loaves of bread and large blocks of cheese? I think it's the latter if I'm being honest with myself."

She stopped speaking for a moment to absorb the words that just came out of her mouth, putting her hands in her pants pockets as a distraction. "Looking quite tan, dark, and handsome today, by the way." Nuru smiled, not bothering to turn his head and instead acknowledging her from the corner of his eyes. Gwendoline's appreciation of aesthetics stopped short of clothing for ideological reasons. "Anyway, I hate that I like social ranks and I hate that I romanticize that era as much as I do. I've been brainwashed by the culture-vulture gatekeepers who continuously prop up and christen the 'master' painters whose work was all influenced by the ruling class as a way to preserve their image and—known or unknown to them—perpetuate the idea that kings and queens carry better genetic stock."

Nuru made a habit of not prying too far into Gwendoline's flamboyant labeling of people or groups, instead deciding to remain silent on the subject until they arrived at the Food Distribution Centre.

The FDC, as it was called by residents of the community within the Hyper Arctic Area, was one of the blue buildings. It was part of the community's PermaPhase-One and its exterior reflected its age. Neither of the two fully understood how the FDC functioned on a technical level, but that didn't stop them from being perturbed that it stuck, even loosely, to a seasonal fruit and veggie program even though everything was grown underground, independent of the Arctic's weather patterns. Nuru picked up some plums, a handful of fiddleheads, and an always-available loaf of bread. Gwendoline didn't get anything, only saying thanks to FDC Maintainer as they left.

"I know I've said this a thousand times," said Gwendoline as they set their course to the floaty things, "but of all the stuff you could do with your time, why would you wanna hang out alone surrounded by a bunch of food?"

"Maybe he likes gardening. Maybe he likes seeing what kinds of foods people are eating. I don't know."

Gwendoline frowned. "I mean, you literally don't have to do anything here. You could sit all day in a climate controlled house and just go to the FDC every once in a while and get food. Why would anyone want to volunteer there? It just seems weird to me."

"Yeah well, a lot of things seem weird to you. Obviously the Maintainer wouldn't do it if he didn't like it. I'm sure my parents wouldn't do all the crap they do if they didn't like it. Although I'd rather do what they do."

"I guess . . . I guess I don't even know why anyone is here at all doing anything if no one needs to be here anymore."

"That's your opinion . . . I guess." He turned his head and looked at the road with a grin. "People like it here. I like it here. You don't have to do anything if you don't want to and everything is provided for you. Seems like paradise to me—if the weather wasn't negative thirty and it wasn't totally dark half the year."

"Yeah, I don't know. I guess you're right." She sighed, killing the conversation until they reached their second destination around eight minutes later.

"Alright, I think I'm finally going to do it," said Nuru. "You think you can get a photo of me in front of the floaty things? I think today is finally the day that I get my picture taken in front of 'em."

"Ha sure, just know that if you think I'm gonna base a piece off of it with you wearing kingly purple, you're gonna be sadly mistaken." Gwendoline was cheery today.

He spoke in his *royal accent*, "I would never ask of you such a favor! Never in thou'st wildest dreams." She knew he wanted one and he knew there was nothing he could do to influence her creative process. Nuru's not-very-secret dream of being the subject of an oil painting was somewhere between a running joke and healthy tension to be kept in place for the benefit of their amusement.

Nuru squatted down next to the floaty things, "I think it'll be even cooler if I increase the distance between my head and the bottom of the floaty things. I think that'll be cool." He was small next to the floaty things, and they were a bit too large to fit completely in the shot. It slightly concerned Gwendoline, the de facto photographer between the two, but humored his impersonation of her concern for the photo's composition and snapped a picture. The image turned out good anyway. Nuru was in the lower third direct center of the picture bookended by four pink monolithic rectangular objects, two on either side, floating about three feet off the ground. Separating him from the objects was an orange plastic fence, the kind people in the far north use for keeping snowdrifts from blocking their driveways and people in arid regions use for fencing off stacks of tires or piles of railroad ties. To the right of the far left pink rectangular object sat the sun, which Gwendoline had managed to fit evenly between two floaty things.

"Wow, you knocked that right out of the park for being such an impromptu thing. Sublime, I'd say."

"Yeah it turned out alright. The tops of the floaty things are kinda cut off but I couldn't really do much about that."

His brows sank for a moment, "Well, now that you say that I'll notice, but I think it looks very good," he said, ending in a smile. "Should we start heading back? I've done what I've wanted to do."

The two pointed back to the livingspace. "Notice how I strategically planned this walk to fall within the golden hour of photography? I knew it would add an element of depth to the photo that would go perfect with the mood the floaty things put me in," said Nuru. He smiled and looked at the far-off mountains.

"You're so fucking full of shit sometimes it's actually unbelievable." She smiled after seeing his smile and shook her head. "Where did you hear that term anyway? Spending more time learning about photography so you can partake in my advanced lingo?" She held the rest of her thought to kick a dirt clod that had detached from the edge of the road. "But in all seriousness, if we stuck around for another four months we probably could catch the golden hour. I'm not sure that's what we would've wanted though.

I think the blueness of the sky would look better than a golden orangey one against the floaty things."

"You're the expert and I'm the novice and I won't dispute that with you," he said, still smiling at the mountains.

They felt the dry wind touch their skin as they walked, a welcome sensation as the oppressive sunlight continued beaming down. In the distance was a different set of much larger monolithic objects which split the sun's light into a rainbow blanketing the warehouse which housed the components that created them. The spires were what the community was known for and it was difficult for residents to go a day without mentioning the objects, even for the younger people such as Gwendoline and Nuru who were more disconnected from their history.

"If I didn't know any better I'd say that those things over there had a refractive index of 2.4168," said Gwendoline, making her voice croak. "Yep, you don't see something like that every day, now do ya."

"Oh I reckin' you're awfully close to being accurate on that there."

"You see that smoke out there though? That's different."

CHAPTER TWO

The two stepped out of the livingspace around 15:00 the next day, forgetting about the smoke. Not much was different from yesterday; maybe the air was more humid, but it was hard to tell. They started walking the same way they always went.

"The wind's coming out of the east today, might be a good day to visit Sinkhole Twelve." The two adjusted their route to Nuru's favorite sinkhole, sometimes referred to as Washerville.

"I wish I could detest more things, but I confess I don't actually know what that word means," said Gwendoline. Her eyebrows were as close to her eyes as she could push them.

"Oh come on," said Nuru in a cheery and half-sarcastic tone, "this is like your tenth day in a row starting us off like this. Why don't you let me start with some weird ponderment of my own or whatever?" Nuru liked hearing Gwendoline's thoughts since she always had things in her brain he'd never considered before. However, last night something happened and it had been bugging him all day.

Gwendoline raised her pitch in faux outrage. "You don't want to know where I'm going with this?" Her pitch returned to normal and she continued, "I didn't really have anywhere to go beyond that anyway."

"I had this remembrance in a dream—or maybe a partial lucid state—last night of something that happened on both my fifth and twenty-fifth birthdays." Nuru glanced over at one of the red houses. "On my fifth birthday, my parents got me a pair of flip-flops with my name printed into them and we ate pizza for supper. I remember being really happy wearing my flip-flops while eating pizza. My parents still occasionally bring that moment up saying stuff like, 'You wanted flip-flops with your name on them so much and I never understood why.' I don't have much of a memory besides knowing that I was intensely joyful sitting at the table. I think some of my memory of the event has been augmented by the pictures my dad took, but even with that said, I was very happy to be wearing those flip-flops and eating pizza."

He took his hands out of his pockets and crossed his pinkie and ring fingers in a snapping motion that would've created noise if done with more force. He repeated the fidget with his hands running in and out of sync with each other before putting them into his pockets again.

"On my twenty-fifth birthday—you were there—I got a pair of hiking sandals from my parents. Last night in my dream or whatever, I remembered them as flip-flops. We had pizza that day too. I remember that because you—rudely, I might add—didn't have any. That was a great day. It wasn't till this morning that I realized how similar the two birthday parties were to each other. Exactly twenty years apart and I can't believe I didn't realize it until like frickin' six months later." Nuru took a breath and glanced at one of the blue houses on the other side of the road. "Is it wrong or right that I see myself as not having changed? I still take pleasure in the same things I did when I was young. I look around and I see other members of our community playing bingo or talking about some piece of media or whatever. Were those the same interests they had when they were younger?" Nuru frowned, starting to look like he was holding back pain from an invisible needle and thread sewing up an invisible gash in his heart. "I guess some people are still brought joy by the same things—a mechanic works on a car he dreamed of having when young. But why for me flip-flops? Why pizza? Why do these items bring me joy? Am I cursed to not be jaded while so many other people around me are? I don't understand it."

Gwendoline sensed his monologue was over. She looked at his face and looked away, staring down the road. "I think you are not cursed," she said, letting her mouth talk for her, "I think there are people who are cursed in the way you're describing—to have interests in activities and objects that do not bring them happiness or fulfillment or whatever. There are, of course, societal pressures to be interested in other things, but I think that even adult things are just kid things operating at a higher level, framed for adults. I don't know."

"Yeah, I don't know either, but it made me tear up a bit today. It was weird."

Some time passed and they arrived at Sinkhole Twelve. Nuru climbed into it following the same path he always took. He passed the skeleton of a sun-bleached four-wheeler before hopping onto a box he assumed used to be on the back of a truck. Clattered together near the bottom of the hole was a pile of washing and drying machines. Three of them were arranged in such a way that a person of Nuru's height could sit comfortably between them as a sort of rigid lawn chair. Gwendoline didn't have a usual spot—she didn't like to sit down when on a walk. At Sinkhole Twelve she preferred to look around at the stuff people had tossed into it. She liked seeing the items people deemed junk. A lot of it was unworthy: vehicles with gasoline engines, lots of lawn mower decks. Neither knew why there were so many lawn mower decks in Sinkhole Twelve. No one in the community had grass and no one, reaching as far back as she could remember, ever needed a lawn mower deck.

She turned to look at Nuru. He was flipping a knob up in the air, letting it gently fall back into his hand. It appeared that his uneasy state had vanished and he'd returned to a more clinical one. He stared forward with his eyes comfortably focused on nothing. It was now safe to bring up something that popped into her head during his story.

"Going off what you said, I think all people regardless of rank or class want the same thing. They all want a bar they can go to and see the same people. They all want people to love them. It doesn't matter if the government gets overthrown. People will be happy as long as they have access to a community that cares about them. The rich people just have a community of a bunch of rich people, operating at a higher level, so to speak."

Nuru pretended to scoff and let the knob he was playing with fall. "Oh jeez . . ."

"I'm just saying that people are going to be equally happy and unhappy at all levels of society but the people at the top are able to have the opportunity to go to bars more often if they so desire."

"I think that's fair. I get that. I don't see how that relates to what I was saying earlier though."

"It doesn't. I just had a semicolon in my brain that connected the two or something."

"Alright." Nuru stood up and stretched before scrambling over to Gwendoline's location.

"Looks like it used to be a fish tank."

Spilling out the sides of the tank were multi-colored pebbles. A viscous medium, gelatinous or otherwise, had congealed many of the pebbles creating a large glob in the middle of the tank. Gwendoline lightly touched a few of the unconstrained pebbles with her fingers. They were smooth and reminded her of washed up glass on the beach, but less porous. They were pink and blue and yellow and green and she snapped a picture. It would be nice to have a reference photo in case she decided to incorporate the feeling the pebbles gave her into a work. It was pretty even as the glob, she presumed, grew ever larger and enveloped more of the loose pebbles. It didn't occur to Gwendoline that the viscous glob could have been, in fact, receding. In any case, it didn't matter which way it was headed. The painting in her mind portrayed it growing larger. The blob wasn't making the pebbles ugly, but rather freezing them from motion, making them unappealing to the viewer in an indescribable way, and yet still beautiful. She sighed and put her camera away and the two climbed out of the pit.

Most of the way back Gwendoline thought about how she could incorporate the pebbles into her next oil painting. Nuru was still thinking about the flip-flops he had when he was five, and about how sad he was on the day that he stopped wearing them. His feet had grown to the point where his heels and toes were hanging out over the edges of the soles. There was tape on one of them from when he had accidentally ripped the "flip" part of the "flop" so the sandal wouldn't stay together. He'd worn them almost every day for a year and a half.

"That dog is barking again."

"It seems to be in the mood to do that around this time of day," said Gwendoline. For a couple footsteps neither spoke. "I think I know where I wanna walk tomorrow but I'll pretend that I don't in order to keep things spontaneous."

CHAPTER THREE

Nuru woke up in the late morning and found Gwendoline in her studio area working on a small painting. It was a portrait of a woman with deep facial wrinkles using her hand to cover the lower part of her jaw. He was well rested and ready to critique the weak methodology he noticed Gwendoline using to paint the portrait. "It looks like you're painting this from a two-dimensional reference image."

"Yeah I know, I know. I can't help it."

"It also doesn't help that the reference image is well known."

"Yeah I know. I'm just trying something."

"What are you trying?"

"Trying to paint something I like."

He shrugged. "Seems like a noble enough cause. Still though. My point stands." In an instant he switched to food mode and went over to the kitchen.

"Actually, I'm thinking we do more of a walk day trip today and leave as soon as we are leisurely able," said Gwendoline, bothered she forgot to mention that before he got out food items.

"I'll just make a quick sandy and toss some water accompanied by various meal powders into my backpack quick then."

"You'd be my personal hero for that."

He started to get some sandwich-making materials from the cupboard above the fridge and sighed. "I'm sorry I keep saying this, but why the fuck did they think it was a good idea to not put handles on all of the cabinets in this place? It's frickin' mid-tier and clearly isn't going for a cool 'mod' look or whatever. Fucking Christ, maybe they built it for a person who had really long fingernails. I don't know."

"Just stop putting the cutting board up there. That's literally the hardest one to open of all of them. Either that or make little tabs out of fabric or plastic and adhere them to the door."

"You think it looks good without handles?" said Nuru, turning around to make sure Gwendoline saw his look of disapproval.

"Well no, I agree with you, but I feel as if you say something similar to this every time you use that cupboard."

While Nuru did mention his feelings about this cupboard often, Gwendoline was an expert at blocking out that the rest of the cupboards were filled with other stuff—a majority of it hers—and she would always veto hypothetical rearrangements.

Gwendoline started putting her art materials into their bins and upon closing the cupboard that housed them, realized she lacked empathy for Nuru's sandwich-making situation. Keeping her paints in an area objectively better for storing food than paint caused her to remember her default memory of painting-related embarrassment. "I don't wanna bring this up, but remember that time I left a couple paint rollers in the freezer thinking it would keep the paint from drying out and it made all the ice cream we were gonna have for root beer floats taste like paint?"

"I was just thinking of that actually."

"I honestly don't know how it was possible for that to happen. I mean the whole container of ice cream tasted like paint. It was like someone—me I guess—had poured mineral spirits all over the inside."

"Yeah . . . fuckin', I couldn't eat ice cream for a while after that. I just couldn't believe that it could actually taste like how it smelled. I regret trying it, but holy crap . . ."

Gwendoline and Nuru both grinned, his more patronizing, and hers a look of somewhat contrived melancholia. "And it all could've never happened if there were handles on the cupboards," said Gwendoline, trying to tie it together. Nuru didn't respond and Gwendoline internally admitted that it was a poor non sequitur. Both refrained from speaking while Gwendoline put on her shoes and Nuru continued packing food for their walk.

The community's air was back to being its normal HyperArctic dryness and relaxed them as they walked. "If I recall correctly, you said you had a destination in mind today?" said Nuru. His cheek twitched from the sun's light and he tugged his backpack straps hoping to forget their need of proper adjustment.

"Yeah, I think it's time we visit the Industrial Centre."

The complex was outside the community about two miles down a private access road that briefly skirted city limits. Paralleling the road was a set of heavy-duty tracks about six times wider than standard train tracks. They walked in the space between the road and tracks. Its mossy surface was composed of browns, reds, yellows, and greens patched together by stitches of purple. As they walked, their feet created occasional impressions into crunchy lichen, reminding them that the quilted ground needed to be washed in cold water in some areas. The sky was par-tially gray and partially blue and a single cloud hung over them like a semi-opaque kite. It seemed to move slowly back and forth when they stared at it. In the distance they could see the Industrial Centre and the diamond obelisks that dwarfed the building.

"I think I know what my next 'serious' painting is going to be. I think it's going to be me standing in front of the spires," said Gwendoline.

"Wow, that sounds suspiciously similar to the picture I had you take of me a couple days ago if I do say so myself."

"Yeah, well, I'm thinking it's gonna be more than just me and the spires."

Without slowing down, Nuru swung his backpack off one shoulder and got out his sandwich.

"You're probably wondering if I put a little bit of Dr. N's Sandwich Seasoning Spread—trademark—on this and I want to let you know the answer is yes."

"Just what I was wondering in fact. But would you dare add the crunch of cucumber slices to that flavor concoction?"

"Why yes in fact, yes I did. Feta cheese? Um . . . ok."

She looked at him with concern, "You know it's dangerous to eat and walk at the same time, right? Like, you could take a wrong step and start choking on a halved cherry tomato and that could be the end of you. If you think that I know how to do the Heimlich, you're wrong."

Nuru was suddenly conscious of each step he took and started lifting his feet gingerly over the rocks. "Please don't ruin this for me. It's a perfect day out here and you're deliberately trying to ruin it for me. All you have to do is wrap your arms around my stomach and pump the thing out. I don't know how to do it either technically but I feel like I could if I needed to."

"Maybe just for safety reasons it would be best to give me the rest of your sandwich then, just so if I choke I'm guaranteed to be saved," said Gwendoline, stretching out her hand for the sandwich. He pulled it closer to his chest and sped up.

They reached their destination around noon, talking about food the remainder of the walk. "I know how much you hate seeing paintings that look like they were painted from a picture, so I brought my 3D system with me to take more in-depth reference photos." Nuru followed her as she moved like a crab in various directions, trying to find the ideal spot for photography. "I think around here is a good place to set up my stuff if you wanna stand in for me so I can get the composition right on this shot." He walked to where she was pointing and stood facing her. Behind him towered rows of the diamond obelisks.

"I'm not sure if you're going for imposing, but I think that's what this pic is gonna look like," said Nuru. "This is some real brutalist shit right now. This looks like some fucking, like, some sort of goddamn place to enter to get your soul ripped out of your body and trapped in space and time. Just think if one of these fell. There'd be a frickin' earthquake."

"I'm not going for brutalist, I'm using this as the basic level for how the overall painting will be composed."

Her 3D photography system was made up of small, identical cameras two feet apart from each other on a foldable grid that, when expanded, stretched eight feet by six feet. The cameras were connected by wires that hugged the grid and lead to a single black box attached to the tripod. "This looks good enough for me. Just to humor you I'll get a pic of you standing there." Nuru smiled, showing his teeth for the picture.

"Alright, you know how to use this, right? All you do is press the button and that's it. You don't need to focus it or anything like that. You don't have to adjust anything. Just press the button."

"I think I know how to press a button." They traded places and Nuru snapped her picture in front of the diamond obelisks. "Oh come on, give me one where you're smiling. That's the least you can do!" She forced a smile.

"Cripes, there's someone coming, goddammit," said Gwendoline. Nuru used the moment to take a picture of Gwendoline's perturbed expression before looking over to see who it was.

"We're not even fucking trespassing for fuck sake, they can't do anything," said Nuru.

"I mean I think you're right, but how the fuck is whoever this is supposed to know that or whatever?" They froze in their poses as the person walked over, their eyes staring, trying to make out the person's features.

The figure approaching was tall and had a wide gait that made him appear like he used to have a powerful stride before back pain caught up with him.

"God, it's some old guy. I do gotta say he's got a very distinguished-looking five o'clock shadow going on though," said Nuru.

"Yeah I agree. He's probably a prick."

As he approached, they could see he was in his mid to late sixties and had brown hair that had slightly desaturated with age. He was wearing two flannel shirts with the sleeves rolled up on the outer shirt, and large circular bifocal glasses with the bottom half taken up for closeups. He was wearing faded gray jeans that, while faded, were still quite clean with no holes or frays. His work boots looked polished within the past week.

"You guys have an ERT permit?" he asked, letting fear seep into them. "I'm just kidding, but what are two young, handsome and beautiful—respectively—people doing way the heck out here?" he said as his face changed from enigmatic to cheerful. "Well, I know the literal fuckin' answer to that, but what motivated you? You see those smoke signals a while back?"

Gwendoline was startled by how fast the man was speaking. Most people in the community talked at a leisurely pace, but he talked like he'd just eaten a habanero. "I wanted to take some reference photos for a painting I'm going to be working on."

"Ahh, we got a feckin' artist over here. What about you?" He nodded at Nuru, giving him an open-mouthed smile.

"I'm not an artist. Just along for the ride today."

"You're not into industrial engineering by chance, are you? Not that it really matters that much, eh? Would you guys be interested in seein' a look inside this little feckin' Industrial Centre that's goin' on here? Maybe a tour? Help an old man pass some time?"

"Sounds good to me," said Nuru without much thought.

"Hell yeah, I've always wondered what was in the Industrial Centre."

"For starters, there's a whole metric fuck ton of industrialness in there," said the man. "I gotta caution you about that. Anyway, pack up that son-of-a-bitch," he said pointing to the camera rig, "and I'll give you the grand tour. I don't understand why this isn't a tourist attraction. Don't people care about this? There are literally thirty-four, thousand-foot tall fucking monoliths made out of pure diamond and you two are the first people even come out here to see 'em up close? It's a fucking fifty minute walk from the city limits for fuck sake. Give me a fucking break..."

He had run out of breath from talking by the time Gwendoline finished packing up her gear. He took a moment to inhale and exhale at a normal pace and then it was time for his grand tour.

CHAPTER FOUR

"Alright, let's start this fucking bitch of a tour," he said, walking backward toward the Industrial Centre. "Obviously it's pretty dumb that we're starting off by going inside when there are literally thirty-four fucking pillars of diamond feckin' towering over us, but you guys see that shit every day anyway I s'pose. My name's Dwaine, by the way." He stopped talking a moment to frown. "Well, my real name is Davyd. Davyd with a fucking *Y* instead of an *I*. I'm sorry, Mom, but I'm not your effeminate little bitch boy. You guys can call me Dwaine. Dwaine with an *I* instead of a *Y*. That's what I go by and what everyone in the community calls me. I feel obligated to tell people my real name, though, in case they ever feel like sending me a gift by mail." He laughed. "No one has yet, but there's no reason to anyway..."

Nuru's eyes flicked to Gwendoline's as Dwaine spoke and were met with a blank stare, "I'm Nuru and this is Gwendoline." Dwaine didn't seem to process the information.

They arrived at the door to the warehouse. To its left hung the curiously small *Industrial Centre* sign, a mid-tier icon of the community. "So before we get started, does anyone have any questions? Actually, you know what? Save your questions for the end. Actually, just ask them at any point. If there were more than two of you I'd ask that you keep your questions till the end but I think we have a good group today." He opened the door and the three stepped inside the Industrial Centre.

"Wait, the door wasn't locked?" said Nuru.

"Fuck no, no one wants to fuckin' come in here to this

goddamn place. I don't even keep the keys to anything on me. No point to that shit. No point at all. Just like there's no point to swearing anymore. Back when I was growin' up you could swear and it actually had an impact on shit. My mom would get angry at me. I could say *fuck*, *bitch*, and *shit* and people would look at me strange and with revulsion. I spent too long with people who all said shit and now it's just baseline. Fuckin' . . . I mean fuck it, whatever. Everyone now isn't offended anyway, so all this swearing just dates me. Whatever, nothing wrong with a little patina."

The warehouse was large on the inside—larger than both Nuru and Gwendoline thought it would be. Dwaine sensed their restrained awe. "Yeah, this bitch is a lot fecking bigger than it looks. You got all this fuckin' diamond everywhere so it makes the building look frickin' tiny. This whole fuck of a place is bigger than five community blocks . . . by surface area."

It was colder than outdoors and they felt a bit chilly even though they were wearing the same amount of layers as Dwaine. He didn't look cold.

"Please note the open concept office layout. This helps with visibility and safety while also allowing a person to throw a fresh fish long distances or see how other people are wasting their time at their desks."

Closest to where they were standing sat a giant box with two large pipes protruding out from one side, taking a hard turn and disappearing into the floor. They were covered in frost which spilled out onto the floor surrounding where the pipes entered the ground. The box appeared to be steel and painted beige with arrays of slits that resembled old automobile supercharger hood scoops.

"I know what you're thinking and you're right." Dwaine

paused, breathing out his nose. "Yes, you do recognize me as being one of the lead team members on the ArctiE-Cat Energy Catalyzer Creation Project, or 'AECECCP,' the project that spearheaded the fuckin' development of the first ever commercially available fusion reactor. No pictures, please."

"Yes, that was exactly what I was thinking," said Gwendoline. "You used to have a mustache back then though."

"Well fuck me hard on a stick and call me stick fucker," said Dwaine in disbelief. He'd actually never had a mustache in his life; he considered himself a tasteful man. "You're probably thinking, 'Oh boy, the first commercially available fusion reactor. That must've been the size of a house!' Well you're wrong. It's just the opposite in fact: the first commercially available fusion reactor was about the size of a medium-sized dog—maybe a three quarters grown poodle—sitting in a Radio Flyer. I mean, not that we used a Radio Flyer—which is the name brand of those old red wagons you know—but the thing was as tall as a dog would be while sitting in a Radio Flyer. Anyway, it was quite small but still put out some good numbers. Thank fuck most of us took necessary precautions and saved ourselves from cancer. I think the reason we succeeded where others failed is that we were using proper PPE. That fed into the idea that if we're going to wear all this shit, we better make sure we're wearing it for a reason. All the other teams never wore proper PPE and I think that's why they never developed the first commercially available fusion reactor." It was hard for Nuru to tell how much of what he was saying was in jest, but Gwendoline correctly assumed this monologue was a part of a memoir he'd never write. "You guys know what OSHA was, right?"

"Yeah, some safety organization," said Gwendoline.

"Fuckin' big shot over here. Yeah that's right. We were fucking spotless. Fucking spotless. Sitting in front of us is the biggest fusion reactor within ten thousand miles. Hell, it's the biggest fusion reactor in the world—at this time. It's a little bit like an iceberg in that there's a little bit more below the surface. My point is that—you people know what HyperFrost is, right?—my point is that this does a lot for the creation of those sculptures outside and for maintaining proper permafrost temperature. There's a lot of fucking weight in and on this frickin' place. We gotta keep the ground artificially cold otherwise shit might hit the fan, and by that I mean that this whole place within a three mile radius would be a giant mud fuck. On the bright side, there would be more sinkholes around."

"So you're saying that the largest fusion reactor in the world is sitting in a warehouse that literally anyone can just walk into."

"Hell fuckin' yeah I am, Nuru." He clapped. "One, people aren't going to come in here, B, what the heck would they do if they got in here? Vandalize it and risk getting heavy doses of radiation? Roman numeral III, you can't steal it."

"Couldn't some knowledgeable team come in and do something with it or reroute some of the underground pipes or turn it off or something?"

"No, there are other ones I'd go to first for that sort of thing. You could hypothetically reroute the pipes, but I don't see what good that would do anyone. Maybe keeping fish you're gonna eat later colder, but you could just dig a hole near the pipes in that case. Yes, the world's most potentially dangerous and powerful device is just sitting here for anyone to tamper with. I've been trying to get the city council to allocate money to a tourism committee. Get people from out of town up here. I offered to build an observation deck on one of the pillars. No can do. Those fuckers. All goddamned asshats . . . wearing their asses as hats. In their defense, do we *need* a tourism board or an observation deck?" He looked at Gwendoline like he wanted her to respond. "Not really, but there's a lot of information that could be spread about this operation and it is quite scenic. Those fuckers. I try to avoid going to the tavern on Thursdays ever since I had an altercation with Jerry, political in nature. Goddamn, that guy's a piece of shit. I live in town but thank fuck it's not near where he's at, and I can stay out here most days. Anyway the cooling system is self-explanatory." He glanced at the pipes and started walking to the next portion of the warehouse.

CHAPTER FIVE

There was another box, this one with many tubes intersecting it and no vents. Beyond this larger box was a circular guardrail that bordered a hole dug deep into the ground. Sitting over the hole was a carbon fiber frame that extended twenty feet up.

"This is all the shit for the CO_2 extraction. My favorite component: the HullBay." He pointed to the unventilated large box. "HullBay? I mean, fuckin', are you kidding me? What kind of proprietary language is that shit? I guess if you made it, you can name it. The unit helps in the process of separating the carbon atoms from the oxygen atoms. It also does methane too but methane is much less glamorous a compound. Its CFC intake days are mostly behind it, apart from what I'm putting into the air."

Dwaine walked backward until he hit a railing and waved a finger down the shaft it blocked. "This is where the science happens. The Big Deep Hole. Part of the creation of the diamonds takes place down there somewhere. Well, it used to, well, I mean there's a different system in place now than there was originally, but technically it all still takes place down there. I don't fully understand it, but that's not my job to understand."

"What exactly is your job?" Gwendoline asked.

"I oversee operations of this place. I don't need to be here, the whole place is autonomous, but I may or may not have set up a clandestine workshop and staging area on the other side of the BDH. Well, it wasn't that clandestine: I oversaw construction and made sure they overbuilt it in case we needed to add another reactor or secondary CO_2 capture system. Obviously I knew we were never going to need that and I had full intentions of using the space myself, so I guess it's up to you to decide if this is clandestine."

"Eh, that's sorta a gray area in my book," said Nuru. "Did you really have to be low-key about it? Seems like you coulda just asked for the space."

"Well you're not *that* wrong, but dealing with these asshat fucks isn't what I would call pleasant. I'm all about keeping things low-key. The less the people know, the better, in this case. Honestly our team coulda requested a facility the size of freakin' twelve of these and they wouldn't've said no. I'm just taking my simple pleasures."

"So how far down does this hole go?" asked Gwendoline.

"It goes down to around five miles."

"And what's it exactly do?"

"Well that's a good question and the answer is not that much at this point. It was used more when all the coolant piping was getting put in the ground. As I sorta said, it was also an older version of the diamond-making process." Dwaine turned around and leaned his stomach against the guardrail. "Fun fact: we may or may not have needed the BDH for diamond synthesis and we may or may not have already engineered a better system by the time this one was being dug." He flipped back upright and his eyes darted to the ceiling. "No, no, I ain't gonna say that. We needed it for the coolant hole-boring process. It would've been harder without it. In any case, there's a giant fucking hole in this building and that's fucking cool."

Neither knew how to interpret Dwaine's words.

"If you follow me to the other side of the hole, we will find the other two thirds of the warehouse full of my stuff." Dwaine's work area looked like a large gymnasium with the wooden floor ripped out and replaced with carbon fiber. Strewn about were two drill presses, a large metal cage with pulleys attached to the top, multiple tool boxes, a car jack, a welding area, several rows of reinforced glass cases, and other objects designed to create and modify things. In the center of the workshop sat a four-by-four arrangement of concrete blocks, each looking to be around three cubic feet.

"As you know, when constructing a building that may require class nine vehicles to enter, you're going to need a staging area as well as all that aforementioned space in case we need to build another reactor." Dwaine grinned in a look of sly triumph, recalling his now-rusty skill of large-scale bureaucratic navigation. "Why carbon fiber?

Wouldn't diamonds make the most sense for this part of the warehouse? Wouldn't that fit the theme better? Why isn't the floor just granite like the other side of the Centre? For starters, diamond is slippery so when you and her—or her and you—wanna pull something out of that giant hole thirty years in the past, you can't be slipping around on diamond. With a nice layer of carbon fiber, we can keep the trucks coming in or out at your leisure. I was advocating to have the entire building made out of carbon fiber and select parts made out of graphene, but they put their foot down on that. Not really sure why considering that all their money was coming from some sort of grant that allowed artistic liberty. I mean, we were forced to display all these frickin' hugeass giant towers made out of diamond but they didn't want the Industrial Centre to look cool too? I mean Christ, corrugated metal painted green and tan for the exterior?"

While Dwaine was talking, Nuru had walked over to the arrangement of concrete blocks and patiently waited for a gap in conversation to ask why, exactly, there was an arrangement of concrete blocks in the middle of the workshop. "This might be a dumb question, but what gives?" he said sitting on top of one.

"No questions are dumb my friend, just ones that are not smart. This is neither a smart nor dumb question, however. It is indeed quite inexplicable that there are sixteen cubes of concrete sitting in what would appear to be valuable workshop real estate. The fact of the matter is that they're something of an art piece I've put together." He beamed at Gwendoline as if to say *Hey, I'm an artist too.* "Back in my youthful years, I helped write a 'concrete and its aggregates' identification guide. The one closest to you,

Nuru, is Trout Rock, known by that name due to a higher percentage chance that one will find agate in the aggregate and for its use throughout the northern Great Lakes region down there to the south and east of us. The one next to it is from an even more exotic location further south. I personally cut it and hauled it out from underwater." He sat on the cube, something in his eyes giving away that this one was his favorite. "Uh, with the help of a crane, obviously. It's called 'beautiful knickknack,' Got its name from the aggregate of shells and that famous tongue twister."

In a mildly condescending lighthearted tone, Nuru asked, "Gwendoline, you think you could critique this concrete sculpture?"

She stepped back to get a better view of the cubes and rubbed her chin, ignoring his condescending attitude. "Off the top of my head, we see an arrangement of what I'm told are concrete blocks from all over the world. Each block created by a different culture for different reasons, and perhaps with techniques discovered independently. These concrete blocks—the foundation of civilization—are arranged together working for the same purpose, the purpose of upholding civilization when one block—or culture—isn't enough. At least that's what I see at first glance."

Gwendoline continued to stare at the blocks. After a moment, she looked up seeking affirmation from Dwaine, even though she didn't need it.

"Hey yeah, that's a pretty darn good interpretation of it. Hell yeah, Gwen. Frickin' fist me on that." He stuck out his arm and they fist bumped.

"The arrangement of the blocks seems somewhat arbitrary. I think the idea would work better if there were some sort of object placed over the top of all of them."

"Ugh, representational art? No thanks," said Nuru.

Dwaine took the momentary pause in conversation Nuru created to jump back in, "These all got used as the models for the field guide. Weighed, photographed, et cetera. I had them shipped up with me when I moved up here. I'm considering using them to build a crypt for myself. I haven't got around to designing that yet, which is partially due to me not having fixed the forklift yet." He pointed to his forklift that Nuru noted was parked oddly close to a buffet table full of pizza-making ingredients. Dwaine noticed Nuru's mental note and grinned. "Have you two ever had wood-fired pizza before?"

"Where the hell do you get wood from?" asked Nuru.

"What kinda question is that?" slapping Nuru firmly on the back, "We're in the freaking Industrial Centre! I make it here!"

"Oh, that makes sense."

"The point being, this is a temporary spot for these blocks until I do something with them," he said, air-quoting the word temporary, "Temporary in that they've been sitting here for several years." He looked at the blocks with a warm smile.

Gwendoline started looking around on her own; she was amazed at all the stuff Dwaine had managed to fit in the Centre. On the opposite side of the wood-fired pizza oven from the forklift sat a partially disassembled pickup. She climbed into the cab and sat on its bench seat, surveying the interior of the vehicle. There was a row of circular gauges on the ceiling and more gauges taking up all dashboard real estate. Where a glove box would've been, there were only more gauges. Sensing Gwendoline's budding interest in the truck, Nuru moseyed over to take a look.

Seeing Gwendoline lose interest in the cubes reminded Dwaine that he hadn't eaten anything so far for the day and hurriedly threw a pizza together, quickly sliding it into the oven so he could to get back to talking. He always had the same toppings on his pizza. It was his way. "That's what I'm working on right now," he said as he rejoined them, "It's a 1985 Ford F250. Redid pretty much everything on it. Fabricated a lot of the parts myself outta carbon fiber. Dropped in a '33 Cummins—the third to the last year they made 'em—and with that had to redo the whole suspension. Obviously turbo'd, will make almost two thousand horsepower and around four thousand pound-feet of torque. All I gotta do is get the doors back on. Still haven't decided if I want power windows or not." He kicked the front tire. "Considering using it to move all those fuckin' cubes one at a time out to wherever I want my crypt to be. Maybe just put in a system based off of container ship cranes. Might ruin the aesthetics of the rig though. I'll have to find out if I can make it look good. Got something similar already modeled up." He motioned to the cage with the pulley system.

"I don't wanna sound like an asshole here, but I'm wondering why you're going to be using a truck that'll be burning a ton of shit into the air when you're also the same person who apparently helped with controlling the atmosphere or whatever," said Gwendoline, more interested in the guy's psychology than the truck.

"Yeah well I figure I'm entitled to waste five hundred pounds of fuel here and there every year. In the long run that won't matter much. The Industrial Centre is doing multitudes of that. Anyway, I don't know where you guys are headed but if you give me a half hour we can take this fucker out and go for a ride. I'd like to get on the doors 'cuz I don't like getting rocks and shit on my pants, but that won't take me too long. We'll leave off the hood and obviously we don't really need any quarter panels." He slapped the side of the truck, "Fuck yeah, this is gonna be fucking great!" Without waiting for their confirmation, he wheeled over a small pulley system to keep the door level while he attached the hinges and got to work. "Make yourself a pizza real quick. I just put mine in. We'll eat before we go unless you guys are in a hurry."

"No, we're not in a hurry," Nuru replied. "Thanks for the pizza offer." He went over to the pizza making-station to see what was offered.

"Where we gonna go in the truck?" asked Gwendoline as she arrived at the station.

"Wherever the fuck we wanna go! Anywhere you guys haven't been around here before? Actually I think you said you already ate but if you wanna make one anyway and bring it with you and have it later, that's totally fine wit' me."

"Well, I'm not sure. There isn't anything that isn't out of my reach that I wanted to go and get a picture of," said Gwendoline. "I think I can't think of anywhere I need to go."

"Ah, well stated," said Dwaine. "Do you know about the cistern?"

Nuru looked over at Dwaine as his attention tore from deciding about artichokes as a topping to an unfamiliar word.

"No, I do not know about the cistern."

Dwaine sensed that neither knew what a cistern was. "You know that thing in extremely old houses in their basements?"

"Uh, I don't think so."

"You know in some toilets, not the ones we have up here, but some?"

Neither responded.

"You ever look at the Archive?" asked Dwaine in a condescending voice reserved only for prime-cut esoteric information.

"Yeah, I'm on there all the time but I haven't ever heard of a cistern."

"You know what the Basilica is? That church or art place or whatever it was?"

"Oh, yeah. I know that," said Gwendoline.

"How the shit are those three things related?" asked Nuru, who decided to put artichokes on his pizza after all.

"Funny you should ask, and I admit there is little to go on based on the gibberish I just spoke'd. Back when we were getting this whole facility designed, we had a team member—who wasn't me—who wanted to include a space where they could go and meditate. Obviously that's a little more of a stretch to ask for. You can't just fuckin' be like, 'Hey, can we build a cistern installed with classical Greek pillars, ornate steps, a mineral bath, man-made hot springs, and marble sculptures spanning from the classical period to our favorite contemporary artists? You can't just go and ask for that. Well, maybe the two of you could, but not a group of eccentric—actually I think wacko is the right word—a group of fucking wacko scientists and engineers don't have the charm and charisma that two young people in the prime of their lives have to ask for that. The point fucking being," he paused to pop a bolt into the door, "that officially it's an emergency air release system or some shit. I can't remember what the heck we called it. Something like that. And it does still function as a way to flush air and/or people out in case of a meltdown. That being said, maybe we did need it. But also that being said, when we were designing the graphene frame that all of this sits on, we included an area for a meditation cistern. We may or may not have included other such areas as well but I can neither confirm nor deny that at this time."

Nuru glanced at Gwendoline who was already giving Dwaine a flash of skepticism.

"Well, that seems a good enough spot as any to go to." She now officially labeled Dwaine as an absolute madman. Nuru had labeled him as one as soon as he saw him wearing two flannel shirts.

"Let's get your 'zas in and scorch 'em a little bit longer and then head out for the cistern. Sounds like a goddamn plan!" He slammed the driver's side door shut in triumph and then slowly jogged to the other side of the truck puffing loudly and keeping his arms in good running posture. "We could also get there quickly from here, but that's the boring way. We'd have to descend into the hole and we'd have to not use the truck. Well we could use the truck, but I don't think things are quite ready enough for that yet..."

Gwendoline and Nuru slid their pizzas into the oven. Nuru went back over to the concrete blocks and sat cross-legged on top of one and Gwendoline explored the workshop, eventually flopping on a couch that was inconveniently located behind a bookshelf. "In about twenty seconds I'm going to need it quiet for the next five or so minutes while I do some wiring shit on this. I'm gonna put power windows on here quick and I'm gonna need to go to my happy place to remember how to do the electronic shit on these motors." That was fine with both of them. "One of you may need to check on my pizza during that time."

Gwendoline tried to have a short decompression session concerning the information she'd accumulated in the past half hour. As she thought, she realized that she was a little hungry too and decided to eat her pizza before they departed the Industrial Centre after all. Nuru, having eaten not long ago, was still planning to save his pizza for later in the day. He wasn't sure when he was going to eat it: he was more focused on the present.

Nuru looked up at the ceiling. It came together like most conventional warehouse ceilings do: at a point in the middle of the building. He looked at the row of cross beams stretching from one slope to the other, reinforcing the roof, and wondered what the person building the warehouse thought of Dwaine. Maybe Dwaine was nowhere to be found during the build and the construction workers never had to put up with him.

Dwaine finished working around four minutes later and the pizzas were ready. Dwaine silently walked from the truck and took them out of the oven and set them at the picnic table. "Who's getting theirs to go?"

"I think I'm going to eat mine here, actually," said Gwendoline.

Nuru scratched his neck. "I'm taking mine with me. I had a sandwich on the way here."

"Suit yourself, boy. These are best when they're fresh out the oven!"

"No, I believe you, I'm just too full right now." In a thought he didn't see coming, Nuru now regretted putting on mushrooms after being conflicted about the artichokes.

He watched Dwaine and Gwendoline eat their pizzas and was surprised at Dwaine's lack of talk. He found it incongruent with Dwaine's personality that he wasn't one to speak constantly while chewing his food. Maybe Dwaine grew up in a wolf pack.

After swallowing his last bit of cheese and crust, Dwaine pulled out a blue handkerchief from his back pocket and wiped down his already clean face. He got up, stuffed it back in his pocket, and grabbed a piece of cardboard which he folded for Nuru's pizza box. "Well, should we be on our merry way? The sun's going to set in five months so we better get going soon!"

Gwendoline glanced at Nuru. The comment didn't amuse either, but Nuru played along. "I didn't think it took that long to see a cistern!"

"Ya got me! It doesn't!" Dwaine smiled: his comment clearly went over well. "It's around a half-hour drive but I bet we can do it in fifteen with the '250. Lemme see if this fucker will turn over." He went over to the bookshelf that was blocking the couch and grabbed a key from the lowest level. The truck started immediately, as he had already tested it, and to Nuru and Gwendoline, its rumble felt like it penetrated their insides.

"Holy sheit!" said Nuru, getting up to walk over to the truck.

"Hell yeah man! What you're looking at is a freaking classic car smashed together with a classic engine smashed together with a bunch of other shit I did to it. Here, help me clear some of this shit out of the way so we can drive out. Dwaine started pushing a bandsaw out of the way with his foot. The two slid the bookshelf and in less than three minutes they'd cleared a path. "I wanna thank you two right now for being the excuse to finally finish up this project," he said, pointing to the pickup, "Well, completing it to where it's fuckin' comfortably drivable. He walked over to the far side of the warehouse and hit a button. The whole back wall started lifting up and Dwaine smiled. "I sure haven't had an excuse to open up this garage door in a while either." He walked back over to the truck and got in. "Alright sorry in advance that there isn't a true 'middle seat,' but I didn't intend more than two people to be driving in this at a time."

Gwendoline took the middle and Nuru handed his pizza box to her before climbing up into the passenger side. "Are we all set? Let's roll out!" Dwaine reached up and pulled a small cord attached to the ceiling neither had noticed and the truck made an extremely loud noise, causing a few screwdrivers and a hammer to fall off the table saw Dwaine moved. "Don't get in the way of this baby!" he said, practically yelling. A three point turn followed by navigating the path at an uncomfortably fast pace, and they were off to the cistern.

CHAPTER SIX

The pizza box sat in Nuru's lap wafting aromas of mild cheese and singed vegetables into his nose reminding him that he had a stomach and it required nutrients. He decided to eat it now on the way to the cistern and have it finished by the time they arrived. He opened the box and its fragrances permeated the rest of the cab.

"Oh Jesus Christ, man, you're gonna make me hungry again!" said Dwaine. "What the hell is this all about? You could've eaten with us! What, it's been like a minute since we left?"

"Sorry, I have no self-control when it comes to food

apparently. You'd think I would've learned this about myself before today."

"I think you've learned that many times but have used your powers of selective memory on that one," said Dwaine. Nuru looked over at him. It was hard to tell if Dwaine was actually angry at him for eating in the truck or if he was joking. It seemed to Nuru that since he opened the box, Dwaine started driving more aggressively.

The ground was still but as they drove its colors blurred together creating a calm feeling within Gwendoline. How similar the ground looked to old impressionist brush strokes streaked together! The far-off ocean appeared and disappeared as they drove, popping up like a sparkling fairy to tease her before she could turn her head to catch a glimpse. The mountains stayed stationary, resembling splotches of brown and gray paint cut to hard edges with a palette knife, disrupting the illusion of impressionism.

"You guys ever do lawn bowling?" asked Dwaine. Gwendoline snapped out of her trance and breathed out her nose.

"No, never," said Nuru, moving a mushroom to the other side of his mouth to respond as quick as he could.

"Nah, no, why would you." Dwaine shook his head.

They kept steady for a while and Nuru finished eating his pizza. A bit after, Dwaine pulled out an object from the sunglasses holder. "Emergency vent twenty-four. Six, Four, Eight, Seven." A light on the dash blinked and a heads-up display appeared on the windshield projecting two lines like virtual windshield wipers. "I like to keep things as close to the original as possible but sometimes you gotta make modifications for the sake of practicality. You guys know what dowsing is? Oh fuck, I overshot a little bit. Goddammit. I don't usually come this way, obviously." He hit the brakes and the truck slid to a stop.

"Yeah, it's some way people used to find stuff buried underground," said Gwendoline.

"Goddammit. I figured no one knows about that shit anymore. Well, can you tell us which way to go based on these divining rods?" He nodded at the two lines projected onto the windshield.

"Yeah, just take a hard left."

"Well shit, this last line of encryption sure as heck didn't work very well." He hit the gas and the wheels skidded against lichen causing the truck to fishtail. Dwaine flipped a switch on the dash marked *4WD* and muttered something under his breath.

"Wait, so why the hell do you care that this location is hidden? You literally don't lock the doors at the Industrial Centre," said Nuru.

"Well, obviously I don't want people going to the cool places," said Dwaine with a look of sarcastic disbelief.

Nuru shook his head. He looked to see if there was a landmark Dwaine was looking for. There didn't appear to be. "We're almost there according to this. I don't know why none of this is familiar." Seconds later he slammed the brakes and the empty pizza box fell off Nuru's lap causing some crumbs and a green pepper stem to spill onto the floor mats. Dwaine glanced at the spill, trying very poorly to hold back annoyance. "Hold on." He unbuckled his seatbelt and his shoes crunched against the lichen as they hit the ground. "Maybe this is actually hidden *too* well." His eyes scanned the vegetation. He turned to face the truck, laughed, climbed in, backed up ten feet, and killed the engine. "Those virtual divining rods work better than I give them credit for." This time, all three got out and stood where the truck had been idling. "See that small-arse fake rock?"

"Yeah, already ahead of you," said Gwendoline, picking up a piece of plastic molded in the form of a misshapen brain. Stuck to yellowed tape on the underside was a bronze key. "Are you serious? A fake rock with a key underneath?"

"Hell, fuckin', yeah!" said Dwaine, relishing each word. "I knew that thing was a good idea. Here, gimme it." She handed him the key, which was heavier than she expected. Dwaine squatted down brushing away some lichen next to where the fake rock had been and unveiled a small keyhole. After a bit of jiggling, the key popped in.

"That is quite possibly the dumbest thing I've ever seen in my life," said Gwendoline.

Dwaine beamed. "I didn't ever think I'd use this fuckin' entrance and doing so with an audience is a real treat. This way, children!" he said, nearly shouting as the sound of roots tearing from the ground surrounded the three. He turned on his heel, still triumphant he'd used the hidden entrance, and marched onto the platform that appeared from under the soil. "There's a lot of controversy in 'the biz' about whether or not elevators should be used in case of emergency. However, being the genius that I am—full disclosure, I didn't design this section—when you enter this way we get to use the elevator. But when exiting in an actual emergency, the whole elevator gets blown out for easy escape access." They followed him onto the platform and he reached down, fumbling around with his fingers, until he found a button which caused the platform to lower.

After about five seconds of motion, the elevator stopped

and they felt wet air whoosh past as the low hum from the sliding door subsided.

"It's, uh, pretty dark down here," said Nuru. They were surrounded in total blackness.

"What, you got a problem with that?" said Dwaine.

"Yeah sorta."

The old man squatted down and brushed his hands against the platform until they heard a *click*. Light immediately started seeping through the ceiling as skylight covers retracted. In front of them they could now see the whole of the cistern. Two rows of Greek-inspired pillars with a pathway made out of marble guided them forward and glimmered as light rays found their way to the water beneath, reflecting into their eyes. The water was seemingly joyous in its newly illuminated motion. The air contained more wetness than what they were used to, yet the air was not wet enough to be what someone outside of their community would call humid. It was pleasant and tasted good in their mouths. Between the pillars stood the marble statues Dwaine had alluded to earlier. The pathway in front of them split into quarters in the middle of the room allowing walks around the whole perimeter, half, or one quarter, allowing them access to the art on the walls.

"You guys can check out the place. There are mineral baths further back and a hot-water-spring-type pool down there as well. I won't blame you for choosing to pass. I think it would be kind of feckin' weird for people to take a mineral water bath on a whim like this I suppose. I guess what I'm saying is that it's open to you if you want it to be."

"Well thanks, Dwaine," said Gwendoline. She stepped out to admire the room. "So this was the vision of a different team member I think you said?"

"Yeah, this was the idea of a person named Darcy. She was into all this type a shit. She was the one who'd come down here the most. She died, I don't know, must be seven, eight years ago at this point? There were five of us working on the project. Of the five, two of us took off to work on other projects when this was done and the other three stayed to oversee for the first years of operation." Dwaine went over and leaned on the center statue. "The two that split died. They both got the plague or something. The other person besides Darcy died at a relatively young age. It was the conclusion of Darcy and myself that he didn't always wear proper PPE when working around radioactive materials. You can only give people so many warnings, ya know. I sorta felt half bad for him, but when it comes down to it, he was a moron." He paused briefly to admire the walkway's shiny surface. "Darcy's death was weird. Not weird as in suspicious, but weird as in weird. It was sort of tragic. She got sick with something. No one officially knew what it was. Something rare. I had a pretty good idea though, I think. I don't know if I could tell you any more about it besides that she was in a lot of pain for a month or two leading up to her death. I don't know, it was sad. Probably a case of improper PPE." Dwaine looked like he was done talking and had dismissed them.

Gwendoline shifted her eyes to the statue Dwaine was leaning on. She recognized it as Hygieia, the goddess of health and hygiene. "So what can you tell me about this one?" asked Nuru. "Besides that there's a guy leaning against it potentially causing structural damages." Dwaine un-leaned himself from the statue and started leaning on the nearest pillar to admire the statue as well.

"Well, she's the goddess of hygiene and we're in a glorified spa right now."

"Ahh, interesting . . ."

Nuru nor Gwendoline were interested in Greek or Roman art at this period in their lives and moved on. Down the way was an abstract piece also from marble. It was a mixture of curved lines intersecting each other, like a half dozen paper clips bunched up with pieces of string running between them. The work was delicate and looked as if it would collapse at someone's breath. "I can tell you about this one," said Nuru. "This is one of those ones that looks cool but is essentially a flex from the person who owns it. I'm assuming that this dates from around the 2020s and utilized *bleeding-edge technology* for all the intricate cut works. This is kind of bogus. All art that is an exercise in skill is. At least to me. This sure isn't speaking to me besides saying, 'I cost money,' but at least it's pleasant to the eye."

"It seems to be that so far we are seeing a theme of opulence," said Gwendoline. "This whole thing—the pillars, these sculptures. It is, however, interesting to note that the people who fronted the cost were not the ones designing and building it. A very low-key flex."

"Maybe it's not a flex at all," said Nuru. "It could be similar to your obsession with baroque furniture but operating at a much higher level."

"Ouch. In any case, there's some interesting psychology going on."

Dwaine walked over from his pillar and caught up to them as they walked away from the statues heading to the left wall. "Looks like you have another guest joining the tour, miss! You think this place is no better than a boy's lust for a fast car? Maybe a girl's dream of a cistern with a bunch of difficult-to-transport art? Well, I guess that's for anyone to decide at this point. I'm sure Darcy could've given me an explanation, not that I ever asked. Perhaps the stuff on the walls will be of more interest to you two sculpture sommeliers."

The first relief was about five feet high and three feet wide painted in full color and set below a skylight. A barcode split the piece in half with a zebra-striped rectangle on top in the foreground. There were three blue circles sitting on the left and right edges of the rectangle and it looked like someone had graffitied the whole piece and drawn a distorted face in the middle.

"Hmm, this one's more interesting," said Gwendoline. "It looks like we're looking at an enlarged computer chip with circuits running from all the different parts of the piece. There is a lot of organic-looking material that was obviously cut by a computer and not molded. That small type serves as text for the sake of text, and the only legible part of the graffiti says, 'Viva people.'"

"What do you make of that?"

"Well, by the look of it there seems to be a lot of imitation going on but nothing is saying anything and there's no obvious implication to the imitation. It's almost as if the graffiti makes the piece whole. Perhaps the artist was trying to make a statement about formalism and that no matter how hard the artist tries to make something a purely visual experience—the closest thing to a perfect idea living only with one's head—the viewer will still see a face, a body, or a pair of arms, and perhaps the face is what actually gives the piece its meaning. Without the face, there are only shapes and color and nature. No

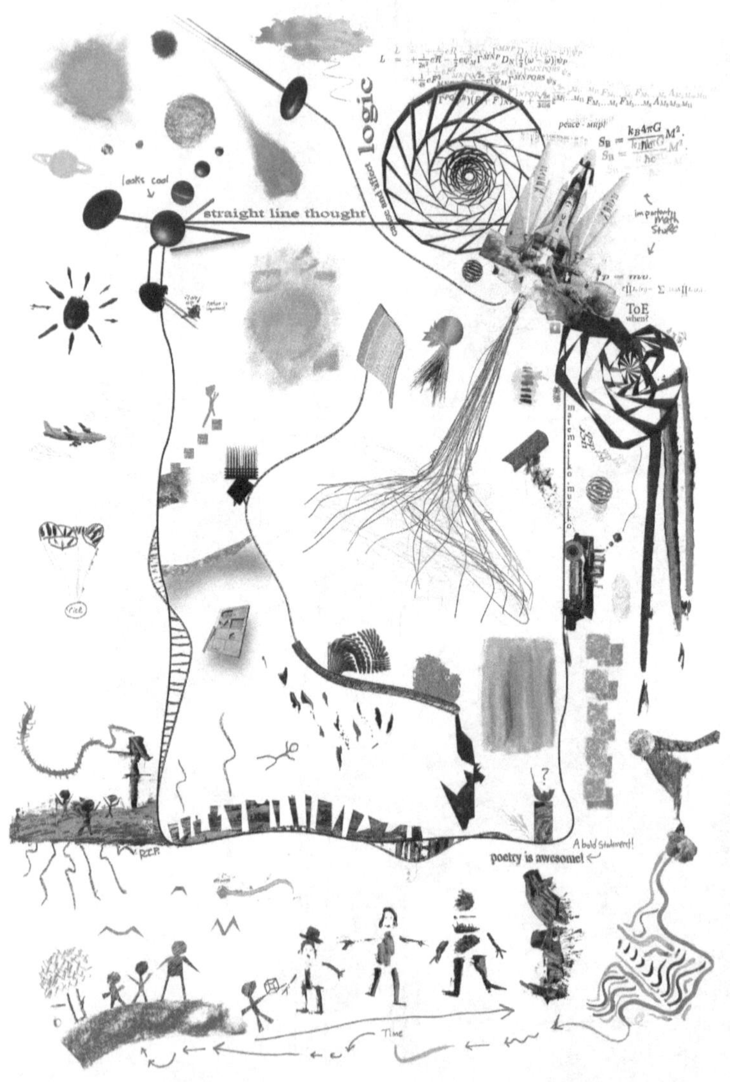

logic
cause and effect
straight line thought
looks cool
peace - miri!
important math stuff
ToE when?
matematiko muziko
poetry is awesome! ←
A bold Statement!
Time
R.I.P.
fire

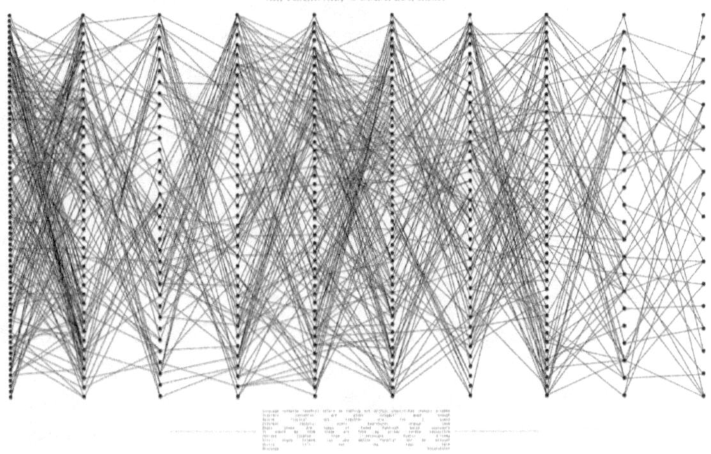

face means no thought nor idea. With the face we see the meaning and the true beauty of the work. The artist 'vandalized' their own work—or that of formalism—to try and convey what the real elements of a work that truly move the viewer are."

"I can't believe I've never taken the time to come over and look at these," said Dwaine. His tone gave the impression that he was joking. Gwendoline advanced the tour, skipping the middle section for now, to a piece that bookended the wall.

"This one looks like it's by the same person. More primitive though. Both composited on a computer and both look to be carved by a robotic arm. This one appears to have pastels, permanent marker, and paper on it rather than just paint. There are two frames." She traced her finger along the inner frame, "Nothing within the inner frame makes any sense to me. Sorta like that last one. The outside is more interesting. The bottom almost looks like primitive cave paintings. The figures—or figure—seem to be evolving into a more and more abstracted state. On the right we see a bulldozer straightening out the lines of the inner frame. To the left we see an aid package being dropped from a technologically advanced aircraft onto primitive looking people. The top shapes look like stars. The top right, mathematical formulas and a spacecraft blasting off." Gwendoline paused for a moment, looking it over further. "This piece seems to want to capture one's imagination but also makes me sad. Within the dreaminess of it, there are what look like poignant themes of the era it was created in, and I guess are still poignant today. Looking at it again, I see a face within this one as well. It looks like an old man with a mustache and he's crying."

"These two seem to fit what I would consider the overall vibe and theme of this cistern," said Nuru. "Knowing how it was funded, et cetera. I mean. Weird that we get shit like these in conjunction with this Greek shit too. Very self-aware. Epic, if I do say so myself."

Gwendoline looked at Dwaine. "You know how these got here?"

"Nah, I wasn't involved with the interior design of this room. Darcy was the art one."

In the middle of the two reliefs were six diagrams, nearly identical at first glance. Each diagram featured four to six columns of dots with lines connecting pairs of dots together. Below each diagram near the ground were lines of small text.

"So what do we have here?" asked Nuru.

"This is interesting." Gwendoline took a step back to take in everything at once. She felt her heel partially dangle over the edge of the walkway and corrected her posture. "I'm thinking that wasting a lot of time in the Archive is going to help me with this one.

"I think I know where you're going with this," said Nuru.

"These diagrams appear to be visual representations of artificial neural networks. That was a big fad when computers were starting to become actually useful. These look like a bunch of node maps."

"Yeah, that's what I'm thinking too."

Gwendoline bent down and looked at the text on the diagram nearest the previous piece.

Intimate Poetry for Untrained Neural Networks
I un-peruse a heterogeneous mixture of thought byproduct
    while it undergoes chemical transformation
Our hips stay touching with my obsolete daywear between,
    stopping fusion
A paltry interaction, your current heat, a local farm's
    tragedy, your current heat
Tired from a handful of strenuous hours, lying collapsed
I fall asleep, my teeth fall out, figures sharing heat
Your heat is mine
My heat is yours,
Shy youth

"Well that wasn't what I was expecting the text to say," said Gwendoline. Nuru squatted so he could read it too. "Wow. Yeah, not really what I was expecting even knowing your experience with expectations. What do the other ones say?" Nuru, still squatting, hobbled over to the next one while Gwendoline was still looking at the first.

Fascist Poetry for Untrained Neural Networks
Wretched beings of fickle muddy pools congeal to form
    civilization
Emerging from the addled yoke are victims of the detritus
Flesh from sludge to soon command the universe
— A confession of vengeful dreams
From fiefdom runoff

"Read this one," he said to Gwendoline, "it's up your alley." He slid over to the next one and Gwendoline took his place.

"This is interesting . . ." she said after finishing the second poem. She slid over to read the next.

Today's Acrostic Poetry for Untrained Neural Networks
Language nonsense (poetry) offers me nothing but drifid,
    unsolicited thought prompts
Ordinary sentences are plumb friggin' good enough
Random "lyrics" put together are fab I guess
Ethereal daylily, comfy heartburn, orange soup
Maybe these are names of faded Pantone® paint colouuurs
It could be that these are from my pricey candle collection
Perhaps cuisine from l"estaurant Fusion d'Yummy
Siri, thyne friend, can you define "drifid" for me please?
Unless it's not une real term
Monsense Miterature?

"This one I'm going to need to think about." She slid over and read the remaining three poems. When she went upright again she felt fluids exit her brain and felt lightheaded.

"Shoulda been squatting," said Nuru, noticing her expression of uncomfortability.

"What do you think of this?" she asked Nuru. "I think I have an idea of what's happening here."

"Seems like based on the titles these are supposed to be for neural networks. I don't know why exactly poems so messy and abstract would be good for a computer though."

"I think that's the whole point. Going back, there was that whole craze in pulp fiction about how artificial intelligence was going to take over the world or what have you. If I was to hazard a guess, I'd say that these are related to that fear. If I think back, I think most of the shit I've seen about it is mostly based on after the computers have taken over the world or whatever. These poems seem to be meant to be data that one feeds into a computer in order for it to become more human. Each poem covers a different theme related to being human, so maybe this was a proactive measure. You feed the computer information to allow it to think and empathize the way humans do so they can empathize with us."

"An interesting take," said Nuru. "Kind of a load of threat inflation if you ask me though. People design computers for specific purposes. Why would they do extra work to make computers more sentient than they need to be? Seems like people were overestimating their own skill level at making artificial intelligence too. I guess we can say that stuff now, but it's not like they could predict the future." Nuru slightly frowned. "What's the deal with the diagrams above them? Clearly they relate somehow to the text since they all seem to be different."

"Looks to me like the diagram is a visual representation of the poem. Each line of the poem has the exact same amount of letters as there are dots in each column. The structure of each poem therefore—wow, a weird implication—each subsequent line uses only letters found in the previous line." She traced one of the lines with her finger.

"Ah, yeah I see that. The poem mirrors the structure of the artificial neural network."

"An homage to the computer, perhaps."

"Showing reciprocal appreciation."

"Certainly an interesting artifact of that era. Makes me wonder what the writers intent was while making this, but also more importantly, how seriously Darcy took this idea." She looked at Dwaine.

"Hell, I don't know. She was into all sorts of shit. Maybe it was just interesting to her. The ignorance of man's view of the future? I'd say that's worth having a reminder of," said Dwaine, shrugging.

"Fuckin' weird if you ask me," said Nuru. They moved to the other side of the room which was predominantly taken up by a large block of text carved into marble and filled in with black paint.

"I think this thing was written by Darcy if I recall correctly. Not sure if it's worth the time to read. That being said, I've never actually read it. She wasn't a tremendous writer."

Nuru stepped to start reading the text, but a small object tucked near the corner of the room caught his eye. Nuru frowned and started fidgeting with his hands. Gwendoline saw what he was looking at too and a bolt of energy traveled through her nervous system. A severed hand on the ground surrounded by some cloves and cumin seeds sat motionless.

"Hmm, I don't think that's supposed to be there," said Dwaine.

CHAPTER SEVEN

The one-handed mayor's dog looked worriedly at his human companion as his human companion sat in the chair. Recently, Louis had noticed a change in his human companion. One, his companion had been late getting his food, and secondly, his companion's body language was starting to make Louis sad. Louis was sad that he couldn't communicate with his friend, and could only understand parts of what his friend said to him. He felt as if he had failed his companion. Louis didn't like this negative energy nor did Louis like to be fed late, but Louis didn't know what he could do. For now, he lay near his human companion and tried not to think about sadness.

The one-handed mayor looked at his dog and wondered what caused the recent change in the dog's behavior. The dog seemed to have less energy this week. However, the thought in the one-handed mayor's mind was merely transient and passed as he moved on to the other thoughts that burdened his brain.

The one-handed mayor lived in a small house, one of the red ones, within city limits. There was, in his living room where he sat, once a wood stove. Some time within the past twenty years the stove had been replaced by an electric heater. The black tubed chimney he'd never bothered to remove hung from the ceiling and lay on the heater chocked by a piece of the heater's facade. Originally engineered as a chintz casing to disseminate heat (and cause accidental burns), it now served to remind the one-handed mayor of his lack of personal initiative. He had two succulents and a miniature bodhi tree that sat in the windows on either side of the front door. The bodhi tree needed to be re-potted. The corner of the room the one-handed mayor was not occupying held a counter braced by cantilevers. The compressive strut nearest the edge of the counter was tragically placed so he could not keep the refrigerator under the counter without it poking out a foot into his living area. In hindsight when adding the counter, the trade-off was not worth its eight hundred pound maximum load. To make matters less feng shui, he couldn't have placed the fridge between the struts nearer the middle of the counter, as the underside of one housed his sink's plumbing and the other, his pantry.

He'd been eating a lot of peanut butter on toast lately. An uneaten piece sat next to him. Tonight he had to venture into the world and acquire more food. The one-handed mayor didn't want to get more food, but he had to. He got up and put the uneaten toast in the fridge before lacing up his sneakers for the trek.

He stepped into the air but turned after two steps, going back into the house to pick up his food bag hanging on the inside of the door. Louis raised his head from the ground as the door opened and lowered it after it closed. The one-handed mayor started his triweekly walk to the FDC, again on the wrong foot. How could it be that he'd continually managed to forget his bag forty percent of the time? He didn't think that thought as he walked. He'd already consciously thought all of the thoughts a person like him thinks. He didn't do anything at his job and he had no power—not that he needed power. His job didn't need to exist and he knew it didn't need to exist. The community didn't need his job. He still had to report to meetings and talk to other people, but it didn't mean anything to him. He was a cog in a system that no longer needed cogs in order to function. He couldn't quit his job and he was missing his left hand. Those thoughts were all old and only occupied space in his unconscious. He rarely had new thoughts, or at least thoughts he enjoyed thinking. Even the conscious topical thoughts seemed to be old thoughts with new names.

At the FDC he remained unhappy. He used to like the homemade bread that a charitable community member brought there, but the taste was old in his mouth and he could smell the dust and the dirt from the floor where the bread was baked. He picked out the other bread, a simple white, much less common for community members to pick, but he thought maybe he'd forgotten its taste. He was deluding himself with hope because he knew that when he bit into it, its taste—the artificial flavor, its sterileness, the cleaning solvent they used on the walls—would be at the forefront of his olfactory recall system.

He was recognized at the FDC as the leading consumer of peanut butter within the community. The peanut butter was old, but it gave him some pleasure that helped keep him alive. He thought of how he would open the top of the peanut butter, stick in the fork, and stir the peanut butter until the separated substances became homogenized. The one-handed mayor was not aware of why he liked the ritual, but psychoanalysis performed by the FDC Maintainer to make his own day go by faster, concluded that it was probably the only part of the mayor's life in which he could output energy and see (and taste) something that looked (and tasted) more pleasurable than before he'd laid eyes on it. Maybe it was for that reason the one-handed mayor would also eat grapes. However, that logic did not logically extrapolate and the FDC Maintainer was incorrect about the mayor's motivation for grape consumption. The one-handed mayor ate grapes because he'd always eaten grapes and no matter how many he'd eaten, he always felt as if he could eat more grapes. However, this was not a grape day at the FDC—this was a bread day and a peanut butter day. Maybe two days from tomorrow it would be a grape day.

The one-handed mayor's walk back from the FDC was how it always was. His eyes glazed in saltwater burning in the wind slowly closed and reopened with the sting returning in an instant. His consciousness thought the tears were from the lashing of the wind, but his unconscious knew otherwise. He stopped when a new old thought of forgotten dog food bubbled up in his brain. He turned around to go back but turned around again to continue home. Louis had enough food until next week. He caught himself slipping up on feeding Louis and experienced a feeling similar to remorse but the feeling quickly slipped into a pool of other damp feelings within his unconscious.

Louis had mixed emotions when his companion arrived home. Louis was excited by the possibility of food, but Louis also worried that his companion was spending too little time outdoors. Louis knew that the outdoors was more fun and more interesting than the indoors and while Louis spent more time with his companion together indoors, he knew his companion would have more fun outdoors, even without Louis's company.

Louis got up to greet his companion, sniffing his lower extremities. The one-handed mayor looked at Louis with a pained smile. The one-handed mayor felt like he needed to smile at the dog, but he didn't feel like he should be smiling. He had the thought of the reason for his pained smile consciously. His brain would soon soon add it to its unconscious. The man went to the fridge and sat down with the now cold peanut butter toast. He had nothing to think about outside of his job and nothing about his job worth thinking. He started eating and Louis wondered how it tasted. It tasted like the dirt on the floor of a house mixed with chemical water. A bit fell on the floor and Louis made quick work of it. To Louis, it tasted wonderful: a good ratio of peanut to bread.

The one-handed mayor looked out the window. He'd not seen the two young people walk by today. That was rare. They'd participated in some events he'd created and he received positive energy from them and had appreciated them ever since. He saw them as people who wanted to experience the world. Maybe since they weren't walking, he'd walk in their place, a good thought he didn't realize he'd had. Maybe it would be good to take Louis out: it had been a while.

He took Louis out into the air. Its dryness felt like it had the power to cut his skin and chap his lips if he moved his body parts in uncommon directions; he wouldn't be doing that though. Louis wasn't aware of his companion's thoughts: Louis thought the air was as perfect as it always was. Louis sniffed the air as they walked and smelled the earthiness of the ground. He smelled a mixture of soil, small scuttling creatures, and the undersides of lichen and moss. Louis smelled the FDC and the home where they made the homemade bread. He smelled oxidized metal and he smelled a very faint saltiness from a body of water. Louis was happy that they were outdoors and walking. He wanted to go past one of his favorite smelling sinkholes. His companion was sure to allow it and that made him excited.

The one-handed mayor correctly guessed where Louis was taking him and walked there in a more angular direction than the dog. He didn't object to visiting sinkholes, although he didn't like seeing them. They were an eyesore, not to him, but to others in the community. The others in the community blamed him for them. They blamed him for everything anyway and they, not him, were the ones throwing their no longer wanted post-possessions into them. Maybe he didn't like seeing anything in the community.

The two arrived at the sinkhole and Louis clambered into it with haste. There were many things for him to smell and newer smells since last time. The one-handed mayor stood at the rim of the sinkhole and watched Louis' methodical olfactory examination of various sinkhole components. The one-handed mayor's mind was blank: he'd already had all of the thoughts related to this experience. Why do dogs like smelling things? Why do dogs eat shit? Why do dogs take so much time before they piss? He'd already had those thoughts. Today he thought about nothing.

After a while, Louis finished his sniffing and they continued the walk. Louis was trying for maximum mileage, but his companion soon turned back in the direction of home and Louis followed. Upon arrival, Louis was in a good mood. He flopped down in his usual spot to take a nap. The one-handed mayor sat down in his chair and frowned.

CHAPTER EIGHT

"Well, what should we do with this?" said Dwaine. He frowned and the bristles of his brow hair almost touched his pupils. "I think this belongs to a living person—it must belong to a living person—I don't think that I heard about anyone dying with one hand or who went missing. You guys haven't, right?"

"No, not that I know of," said Nuru. Dwaine seemed to have sprouted more wrinkles on his forehead since Nuru last looked at him. The old man moved his eyes and body away from the hand looking for more body parts but the cistern's floor appeared entirely vacant as he checked the mineral baths at the back of the room.

"You guys don't know anyone with one hand, do you?" said Dwaine, his voice bouncing off the walls and finding its way first to Gwendoline's ears.

"Not that I know of."

"Yeah, I sure don't either," said Nuru.

Dwaine peeked into the calm waters of the mineral baths. There was nothing abnormal but faint discolorations around the pool walls where the water met the air. The hand was the only foreign object present in the room. Dwaine faced the two from the baths so his words could travel directly to them. "Who the shit has one hand here? I guess it could be some person from not here, but I think the odds of that are astronomically low. I sure as fuck don't know anyone with one hand." Dwaine was technically wrong: he knew the one-handed mayor but didn't know that the one-handed mayor only had one hand. The one-handed mayor wore a very convincing prosthetic in public. In fact, very few people in the community knew the one-handed mayor had it.

Dwaine still looked anxious as he walked back over to the hand, but the boomtown of wrinkles on his forehead was gone. "Well I guess we'll just fuckin' leave it here."

"Really? Shouldn't we alert someone or something?" said Nuru.

"Uh, I don't know. You think that's needed? I don't know if that's needed. Let's just leave it here and I'll take some pictures of it and see if I can find out whose hand it is."

"Alright I guess," said Nuru, his voice implying a physical shrug, "I don't really have any better ideas. I don't know who we could call about this."

Dwaine kept running through everyone who this hand could've belonged to but the list was short and all included were either dead or had hands. He'd known for a fact that all of them had hands when they died. It was impossible that someone could've dug up a body and cut off a hand and placed it there. That didn't make any sense, not that any of them knew how to tell if the hand had been cut from a living or dead person. The only explanation that made sense to Dwaine was that someone unknown to him knew about this place. That, or one of the few people who did know had transported a severed hand here for some reason. He hadn't actually visited the cistern in a long time.

"I mean, I just don't fuckin' want people to know that this is here. I'm not trying to cover up some crime I've committed. I would've done a better job, believe me. I ran through a list of people and my final thoughts are that this person is alive and wasn't a member of the group out here. Seems like getting to the bottom of this is in our hands." He paused. "I didn't mean it like that." Dwaine snickered and continued. "Well, it's also not your responsibility. It's just a hand and there's a good chance that the person is still alive, or at least wasn't murdered, and there may not even be any wrongdoing. I don't know. You two shouldn't feel obligated to get to the bottom of it. Fuckin' obviously since I'm the last one still alive that knows about this place, this would be my responsibility. And even then, I don't think it's dire. I think I'd've heard something about this if it was important." Dwaine stepped away from the hand, looking around at the rest of the cistern in case he'd missed something on the walk over to the mineral baths. "I'm feeling kind of weird suddenly," he said again. "I'm thinking we should pack this trip in. This whole hand thing is bothering me and I'm getting hungry again."

"You thinking of trying to figure out whose hand it is?" asked Gwendoline.

"Yeah I don't know. Honestly I think it'll be essentially too much work just to satisfy an itch. I've satisfied a lot of itches, honestly more than any one person probably has needed to, so knowing me, in three or four days I'll have put this behind me. Not to say that I won't be checking out people's hands and arms when I'm socializing or shit like that, but I have other itches I need to scratch before I die or whatever, ya dig?"

A half-wince flickered over Gwendoline's face as she was unable to discern Dwaine's level of honesty. He seemed uncomfortable, but was that due to him covering something up, or him being afraid of seeing a severed hand and thinking the two of them would be suspicious of him? At the moment, she was giving him the benefit of the doubt, leaning toward the latter.

"So did we come to a conclusion on what we're going to do about the hand?" said Nuru. He leaned against the marble wall displaying the folktale and felt his shoulder fill the slight depressions where text had been carved.

Out of the corner of his eye he saw the words *Mr. Beaver scuttled* which made him temporarily lose his train of thought.

"So there are no authorities here who seem like they're going to come and collect clues, not that you'd let them in here anyway," said Gwendoline.

"Goddamn straight I wouldn't."

"So here's my proposal: we take some pictures of the hand in its original spot, and then I take the hand with me."

"You want the fucking hand?" Dwaine snorted and a bit of crust dislodged from the roof of his nostril and got caught by a nose hair.

"Well yeah I want the hand! When and where else am I gonna get another chance to have a severed hand?"

"What the fuck are you planning on doing with it? Outside of this climate-controlled environment it's going to start decaying and might start to smell or some shit." Dwaine felt the imbalance of weight in his nose, pulled the nose hair out, and flicked it to the ground.

"Eh, it looks like it's close to done doing that. I can throw it in a sealed container or run it through a dehydrator maybe," said Gwendoline.

"Well does this hand really belong to us though? Seems to me like we should try and return it," said Nuru.

"Well I'm not saying we shouldn't, I'm just saying that it might need to be dehydrated anyway before we give it back."

"I don't know too much about hand preservation but that doesn't sound like how one would go about preserving a hand."

"I don't fucking know, we can cross that bridge when we get to it."

"Eh, sounds good to me," said Nuru. Gwendoline walked over and gingerly picked up the hand.

"I got a bunch of bags in the glove box," said Dwaine as he started moving to the exit. "Just when you thought you'd seen it all." He shook his head and pressed the button leading them back up to the surface.

"Oh good, looks like the truck's still here," said Dwaine. "This has been a fun afternoon, I'll say that much." He looked up at the sky so his eyes would adjust faster, not caring about the burning sensation it created. "You want me to take you back into the city limits or back to the Industrial Centre? If you guys want, you can make another round of wood-fired pizzas." He walked over to the door and entered the truck looking exasperated.

Gwendoline mirrored his movements on the passenger side. "That sounds good but I'm not really into the same food item two times in one day."

"I have no problems doing pizza again, but out of solidarity I'll side with my friend on this one." Nuru got into the truck and slammed the door. "What a satisfying door-close sound . . . I think you can take us to the Industrial Centre and we can walk back from there—I don't want the townsfolk's first impression of your new truck to be less than amazed." Dwaine picked up a tone skirting snideness from him but he'd misheard over the rumble of the engine.

"Good point, the people should only see the rig when it's all put together."

"We both like walking so it's not really a problem. It's almost like a hobby," said Gwendoline. Dwaine looked around before departing, his eyes darting as if still searching for something distant in his mind. A moment later they jolted forward and arrived back at the Industrial

Centre seemingly faster than the trip out. When they arrived, Dwaine pulled the truck back into the warehouse and made sure to remind them to not leave the hand in the glove box. Soon after, the two started their walk to the community.

They closed in on the livingspace around 17:00 with most of their thoughts revolving around the hand's, to all appearances, deliberate placement below the folktale. However, when they stepped indoors, clouds of supernatural speculation subsided.

"So," said Gwendoline, "we sorta gotta figure out whose hand that is—whose it used to be."

"Do we?" They looked at each other for a moment, Nuru's eyes falling down to his backpack. He took out the hand and set it on the coffee table. It was hard to tell if the hand had come from an elderly person or a young person, but it was definitely aged. They stared at it without saying anything. It was a deep bronze and its fingertips looked swollen as if it had been poorly vacuum packed. Its skin was yellowed and looked brittle and stiff. However, the longer they looked at it, the less revolting it became.

"What was Dwaine saying about that guy who he didn't like? Something about how he couldn't go to the tavern on Thursdays?"

"Yeah, Jerry. At the very least he'd be able to give us a feel for Dwaine. He seemed like he was being honest with us, but on the other hand, any time someone's being that cheery, it could be reason to raise the red flag."

"Maybe cheery isn't the right word, but he was certainly something."

"I guess we'll just have to swag on over to the tavern on Thursday and see what this fabled Jerry is up to. If it's anything like I think it will be, we'll be in for a big can of worms. The worst kind too: worms that are into local politics."

"That's how it sounds to me. Anyway, I wanna see how these pictures turned out." Gwendoline got out her camera rig and transferred the data onto her personal computer.

"These look alright," she said, flipping through the images. "Goddammit, that last one you took with me looking worried—real nice."

Nuru smiled slyly. "They say the best pictures are always candid and in the moment." He flopped down on the couch.

"It's taking my fullest mental energy to not delete this terrible picture of me but I know that it *is* the best out of them." Gwendoline looked at herself, worried, looking sideways as the mysterious man in the background approached, the towers of diamond in the background shining a small rainbow of color onto the ground. "This would change the tone of this painting I'm trying to eventually make quite a bit if I used this as the base. . . . I'll need to think about it." She flipped the picture off the display and walked over to the fridge. "That was some good pizza but what to have for dinner?"

"I don't know what I'm gonna have. Shoulda taken up Dwaine on his offer now that I think about it. Did it seem like after we found the hand he tried to move us along?" Nuru frowned and got up from the couch after catching a whiff of the hand's post-putrefaction.

"Yeah, I got that impression. I just wonder what the reason was for that. Finding a hand would freak anyone out and I guess finding one in an area that he thought was hidden would also come as a surprise."

Nuru went over to one of the cupboards and got out a food storage container. "Who knows, I find it really hard to believe that he doesn't know whose hand it was or that there was a hand down there." Gwendoline found nothing satisfactory in the fridge and turned around to watch Nuru plop the severed hand into the plastic container. "I'm thinking that if he knew it was down there he would've removed it, so I'm thinking that he didn't know it was down there. If he chopped someone's hand off, I can't see him or anyone leaving it there. Just a single hand? I mean, come on. I'm pretty sure he didn't know it was there or else why invite us down there?" Her eyes tracked the hand as it hovered over the ground toward her as it found its way into the refrigerator.

"Maybe he wanted us to find it with him," Nuru mused, half joking but half serious.

"Why the fuck did you put it in the fridge? It's been sitting at room temperature for all its life probably. At least put it in the freezer." She looked at Nuru searching his face to figure out why the refrigerator preference. "You're saying just wait for years until a person or people come wandering out there and invite us to some weirdass place with a hand? That would be really convoluted to me."

"Who knows, it seemed like he was a pretty convoluted dude. He mentioned smoke signals too." He moved the hand to the freezer without contest.

"Yeah, but what's the endgame there? Is he getting some sick kicks from watching us see a severed hand? I don't imagine that's the case. He's gotta have his own theory about how it got there. There's no way he isn't like eighty to ninety percent sure what happened."

Nuru opened the fridge again. "I think I'm just gonna

have some almond milk and retire to my chambers. I'm considering doing some research in the Archive about some of the shit Dwaine was talking about. Probably will just end up reading about those hundred year old trucks or whatever we were riding in today. I'm guessing those weren't made completely of carbon fiber when they debuted."

"Alright, have fun," said Gwendoline, "I think I'm gonna brainstorm about some art thing I'm thinking about and then go to bed. Who knows if that's how things will play out. Probably not."

CHAPTER NINE

Right after the two left, Dwaine started circling around the Big Deep Hole thinking about the hand. He knew he had nothing to fear. He didn't know whose hand it was, and it certainly had not been he who severed the hand. He should've felt at ease knowing he was guilt free, but alas, he could not. "There could be a chance that—nah—there's nothing to uncover," he said to himself. For a moment he considered inviting Gwendoline and Nuru back to explain to them what he knew, but that wouldn't make anything clearer. He stopped pacing for a moment and looked down into the hole. "This is where things start to fall apart for ole' Davyd." He felt something within him. He felt a pinging in his chest as if a butterfly with tiny needles attached to its wings were fluttering around inside him. He stood up on top of the safety railing and tried to see how far down he could look. He felt his heart jump up into his mouth as he momentarily lost his balance. He stepped down from the railing and felt his head clear up and his body relax. He would think more about the hand later.

CHAPTER TEN

It was Thursday. Between the day they visited the Industrial Centre and now, Gwendoline and Nuru had accomplished very little. In fact, the only thing they'd done is switch up their walking route. This route change came with the intention of giving Gwendoline a fresh perspective with which to see events as they took place within the community. Nuru was skeptical this would have any effect on finding the former owner of the severed hand, but played along as there wasn't any harm in it.

Their new route caused them to no longer pass the one-handed mayor's house. The one-handed mayor wondered if the two had stopped seeing each other. Maybe they weren't even a couple to begin with. He supposed it was none of his business. They were both approaching the age where they would qualify for their own building, but maybe they enjoyed squatting together at FiveLab in order to get away from their parents. He was acquainted with both sets of parents and they seemed like normal people. Whatever had changed, he hoped they were taking good care of the space. It was never easy to find someone who wanted to clean out vacant buildings, and most of the time the task fell to him.

Something felt odd not seeing the two walk past his house and he started taking walks on their behalf after his test walk with Louis was so successful. Maybe it was an excuse for the one-handed mayor to get out and walk:

maybe he thought his dog looked antsy, but he'd walked every day since they'd stopped appearing. The one-handed mayor did not fully understand his actions, but started to enjoy going out for walks. Louis did too. His companion was starting to look better and Louis thought that walking would have nothing but positive effects for his health. He was not wrong and that made Louis happy. Even in the few days that the one-handed mayor walked, he noticeably had more energy. The one-handed mayor was even considering entering the community's social scene tomorrow and engaging with the socialites he'd sanctioned public space for. He still hadn't decided. One of the next few days he might . . .

*   *   *

Gwendoline and Nuru were preparing to engage with a singular socialite known only as Jerry in hopes of seeing if they could get a reading on Dwaine. They left the livingspace around 15:30 and headed on foot for the bar.

"So do we let it slip that we found a hand?" asked Nuru.

"I was thinking about that." Gwendoline kicked a dirt clod as she walked. "What I'm thinking is that we don't, but maybe ask some questions that could lead him to answers that would allow us to figure out if he knows about it. Better to keep things on the DL. Rumors'll spread frickin' fast and we won't ever get a chance to get to the bottom of this before someone goes into hiding or whatever."

"Well do we really *need* to get to the bottom of this?"

"Well no, but what else do we have going on?"

"Yeah, good point."

They walked in silence until the tavern's chimney poked out from behind a blue house. "Ok so how do we know who Jerry is and how do we even know that he's going to be here at like fifteen hours?" Nuru looked at Gwendoline for an answer but she was still occupied spotting loose clods of dirt.

"What I'm thinking," she finally replied, "is that we just ask the bartender and the bartender'll tell us which person he is. There's gotta be only like three people in the place anyway right? Does anyone actually come here?"

"No, I don't think so. Only old people and people trying to deliver limbs back to their rightful owners pretty much."

The tavern was made from coarse lumber and treated with a light matte finish, giving what would be the appearance of freshly cut timber—if the building wasn't covered in a thin film of dirt that looked like it had been sitting on the wood for dozens of years. In fact, it *had* been sitting on the timber for dozens of years. No one had bothered to wash it since the regulars didn't care what it looked like. Its blue metal door looked to weigh at least 150 pounds and was possibly salvaged from the wall of a building that no longer stood. It swung open easily. The interior of the bar wasn't much better from the exterior except that instead of dirt on the walls, there was dust. The ceiling was covered with dust that stuck to the wood shavings that never managed to peel off when the trees were cut into slabs. The same was true for the walls, but to the building's credit, most surfaces frequented by regulars were sanitary. Since this was one of the few unplanned and unsanctioned buildings, it did not have an air filtration system so the air was stuffy and felt too warm. It was dim and there was faint opera music floating in the background, unfortunately still able to cut through the heavy air. The bartender grinned and put down her needlework when she saw the two walk in. "What the hell are you two hoodlums doing in here on such a nice day!"

"Oh shit!" said Nuru. "I didn't know you hung out here!" He half smiled as they started walking to the bar.

"Well now you do," she said, opening up the countertop flap to meet them halfway.

Sarah had been good friends with Nuru but especially Gwendoline when they were very young. They'd drifted apart after Sarah's family temporarily moved away from the community for unknown reasons. They'd heard Sarah was back, but didn't know where she was living or how she was spending her time. Nuru didn't know her nearly as well, but Sarah was the type of person where that didn't matter. She talked to everyone as if they were good friends.

"You got back here about eight or so months ago?" said Gwendoline after finishing their hug.

"Yeah yeah something like that. Things are weird you know. First I thought I'd be gone from here for six days and then that turned into almost a decade and then I thought I'd never be back, but here I am!" Gwendoline didn't know how to proceed with Sarah. In theory they had a lot of catching up to do but Gwendoline wasn't interested. She didn't know why she felt that way, but she did. Maybe the length of time had made their memories so faded that she no longer felt the emotional connection that used to exist.

"Say, is that guy over there playing cards with that girl, Jerry?" she said as she performed a quick snap of her arm in the direction of the two people at the booth.

"Yep! Jerry and Sarah—not me—but her name's Sarah too!" She spoke excitedly but her face told them she'd consciously made the effort to be quiet enough to make sure they didn't overhear. "They come here every Thursday like clockwork. Actually, It's almost exactly like clockwork. I swear they're always within thirty seconds of the top of the hour which is fifteen hours in this case. You meeting them for something?"

"No, we're cold calling them I guess you could say. A person we met recently threw out his name."

"Ah, okay, I see. Still a supple and inquisitive mind, you are!" Sarah smiled but then her face sank. "Wait, does this," she paused, putting her hands on her hips, "does this mean you didn't come to see me?" She smiled again affirming that she was only joking and also because her frown had amused herself.

"That was actually the second reason we came. We heard you make the best highball cocktails in a thousand miles."

"Funny, I'm probably the *only* one making them in a thousand miles." She put her hand to her heart pretending to be flattered.

"Actually, don't forget the people making them themselves," Gwendoline added.

"The best highball maker in a thousand miles operating in a public space then!" said Nuru.

"That has quite the ring to it!" Sarah was smiling quite hard, almost beaming. "But I don't want to hold you guys up any longer than you need to be." She leaned over putting all her weight on one foot. "What are you'll guys drinking tonight?"

"I'll take some neat bourbon."

Nuru had to think for a second. "I'll have a scotch and soda—your famed highball."

"Sounds good to me!" Their choices didn't sound good to Sarah. She preferred drinking mostly wine. She couldn't stand the taste of most spirits but couldn't bash the two since most community members also had poor taste. She ducked under into the bar and hastily made the two drinks, spilling a lot but not seeming to care. "There ya be!" She smiled. The warmth of her smile mixed with the warmness of the air mixed with the warm color temperature of the lights created a feeling momentarily too warm for Gwendoline.

"Thank you much, Sarah. We'll have to catch up some time when we're not on *official business.*"

"Any time now, I got more of those where that came from too so if you run out come back over and see me!"

"Sounds good!"

They turned away from the bar to Jerry's table and Sarah went back to work knitting.

"Excuse me, I hate to interrupt your guyses game, but are you Sarah and Jerry?" asked Nuru. Jerry looked up from his hand and surveyed the two. "That depends on who's asking, I suppose," said Jerry. His otherwise handsome face was vandalized by a cocky grin.

"Well we already know you're Jerry but I'm Gwendoline and that's Nuru."

Jerry smiled again. He had dimples when he smiled that made him seem younger and more attractive than he was, both internally and externally. He was mostly bald and wore a plaid shirt with something in the front pocket which neither of the two could make out. It looked heavy. Sarah was much better looking than he. She had a cheery face framed by long hair which curled down nearly perpendicular with her shoulders.

"Well how come you know us but we don't know you?" asked Jerry.

"That would be because we're not regulars of the tavern and we're also about thirty-five years younger than you. As far as how we know you, it's because we know a person who is your age named Dwaine." Sarah took a sharp breath making a subtle *here we go again* face.

"You two better pull up a couple chairs real quick. What's that rat bastard told you about me? I hope he hasn't been filling your brains with half-truths and half-wits." He motioned to some chairs sitting at table near their booth. "Well I suppose we're done playing Go Fish for the evening unless you two want to join us."

"I'd be interested in playing a game or two," said Nuru in an earnest voice but hoping they'd put the cards away. Gwendoline had no interest in playing Go Fish and for that reason said nothing.

"Well we're not playing anymore while you guys are sitting here. I can't focus on more than one thing at a time and especially if I have to defend my reputation from Dwaine." Jerry was somehow smiling and scowling at the same time. He started putting the cards away even though they were mid-game, probably an excuse to start a fresh game as Jerry was badly losing to his wife.

"You don't have to defend anything—we're just trying to get the scoop on the local lore."

"Yeah, I'm sure I don't. Two young impressionable minds hearing directly from Dwaine about me. I can guarantee it was nothing good."

At this point Gwendoline understood that he no longer harbored bitterness from whatever came between Jerry and Dwaine. From the interaction thus far, she read that Dwaine was someone whom Jerry simply liked talking about. Jerry's Sarah looked down at her near-empty glass and drank the rest of its contents.

"Hey other Sarah," she said, turning halfway to the bartender, "can you fix me another one?"

"Sure thing, Sarah!"

"First of all, how did you two meet Dwaine?" said Jerry, taking a quick sip of his brown liquid. "You must've been at the Industrial Centre for some reason?"

"We went out to take some pictures by the diamonds and he came outside and talked to us," said Gwendoline. Jerry looked at her with skepticism so she continued. "I'm a painter and I wanted to take some reference photos for an upcoming work—kind of an amalgamation of things related to myself and the community."

"Interesting."

"So he just came out and started talking to us pretty much."

"Well, more like talking at us," added Nuru.

"That sounds more like it," said Jerry nodding in approval. "I'll tell you one thing right now: Dwaine is a card," he paused for a moment, "but he can be dealt with." Jerry's wife leaned back and cracked her neck using the back of the booth.

"The story you're about to hear is quite good, but please forgive me if I seem bored or disinterested while he tells it," said Sarah. "I've heard it approximately forty-five to fifty times."

Jerry looked at Sarah with a moderately stupid grin. "I'm sorry in advance but this story is too good and I'm sorry that you're going to have to hear it again."

"I'll make sure you get all the details right." Sarah never actually made sure of that. She found it more rewarding to keep track of which details changed and what parts were left out. There was always something Jerry'd miss.

"So you guys want to know about Dwaine, huh?" He

leaned over the table as if the lights suddenly dimmed with an expression that made him look as if he'd just donned a porkpie hat. "I've lived in this community almost my entire life, I grew up here, I went to school here, I lived here. I, like many others, took some time away from the community when I was in my twenties to see what else was going on in the world, but I've spent a majority of my life here. Dwaine did not grow up here. He . . . is what I would call a ringer. They brought him in to fix a problem because he knew how to fix a problem. He doesn't mesh with the community and has made no attempt to do so. And I don't say that lightly. In fact, I arrived at that con-clusion after a dealing I had with him." Jerry snapped out of his fake trance to see if he'd hooked the two, but they did not seem fascinated, at least not yet.

"A while after he came here and the Industrial Centre was built, the community had a thing where we wanted to repurpose this one house. He came to the city council, which I was on at the time—still am—asking if he could knock it down and build a new building that he claimed would be a place where people could come and get ice cream. He said that the whole thing would be automated and that it would be the best ice cream that anyone's ever had. We told him we'd look into it and see if the neigh-bors thought that would be okay. Obviously we had to check if anyone had allergies, et cetera. He got a little antsy when we said that, put up a little fight. Ultimately he caved and stopped yapping about the check we said we had to do."

Sarah sipped her vodka lemon; Jerry usually mentioned how Dwaine would pound his fist on the podium at the council meeting.

"So I somehow drew the short straw and had to go out and ask the neighbors—this was in an area with a lot of residentials—if they'd be alright with an ice cream place being built near them. Most of 'em were indifferent, one person had an allergy to ice cream, and one person guessed that the person behind the ice cream place was Dwaine and insinuated that the ice cream place would be a front built to spy on them. The person—whom I will not name—said that they worked on building the Industrial Centre—one of the few local workers—and got into a lot of arguments with Dwaine about stuff. See, this worker caught on that Dwaine was taking resources for the project and putting them toward a bunch of other vanity projects. Now, this kind of stuff happens all the time. I for one have employed the same tactics, but not everyone appreciates it. So this worker confronts Dwaine about a room they're working on, saying something about how they don't know how it's important to the overall project. Needless to say, it ticked Dwaine off quite a bit. Dwaine and them essentially start feuding. Unbeknownst to me, I find myself in the middle of a cold war. I mean, I don't think this worker had any intention of telling anyone that Dwaine was using funds inappropriately, I think Dwaine was just a hardass who'd pissed off that worker too many times. So the worker threatens to blow Dwaine's cover—issues an ultimatum—pretty much trying to provoke Dwaine just to make him angry. Suddenly zip-de-dip."

Sarah took a drink.

"Dwaine was trying to build an ice cream place so he could install surveillance devices as close to where this worker lived as possible. I didn't doubt the person for a second because from how Dwaine acted at the council meeting, it seemed like something he'd do. So what do I do?"

He paused as if genuinely asking Gwendoline and Nuru for an answer before continuing without letting them give one.

"I tell him, at the next council meeting, that the council found that there was a person with very bad allergies living too close and that it wouldn't be possible. You better bet that he had a backup plan ready for that. He, without even blinking, takes out a plan for a soft pretzel place. Right away I knew the worker was telling the truth even though I already knew they were anyway. Absolutely stunning. This guy actually was willing to go to the length of designing a soft pretzel place instead of an ice cream place just so he could spy on someone. So anyway, then the council asks him, and I'm the one who is speaking—so I bear all the blame of course, lucky me—what kind of equipment he would use for making the pretzels. He talks about some state-of-the-art machine and all it can do, and then I tell him that we would have to rezone the plot of land for commercial use due to the nature of the equipment and we'd have to ask people if they had allergies to wheat. Oh, obviously he couldn't have just assumed ownership of the house either since he already had a place within city limits. So this community advancement endeavor was his only option at owning multiple buildings. So I tell him that we'd have to rezone it and that that process takes anywhere from eight to ten weeks. He gets visibly upset and now thinks that I must be in on it. I don't care what he does, but I'm not letting him just build a soft pretzel place out of spite. Did the land actually have to be rezoned? Technically, yes. But did it actually take eight to ten weeks? No it didn't. I'd discussed this with the council beforehand as well so they were on board with me saying that." Sarah took a drink.

"Anyway he got really angry and started asking about ways he could accelerate the process. Unfortunately there was nothing we could do." Jerry shrugged and followed it up with a quick smile. "So then, to make a long story short, things escalate and it gets *loud* in the council chambers. Dwaine tries to pick up and throw the podium toward us. Keep in mind, the podium is made of super dense hardwood. He gets it off of the ground and yells extremely loud and the podium moves maybe six inches toward me. He storms out and it looks like he's in severe pain, all hunched over like. Get this." Jerry paused and slowly moved his eyes between Gwendoline and Nuru. "A friend of mine sees him at the hospital the next day, turns out he gave himself a hernia." Jerry shook his head, grinning. "Never saw him again."

Sarah took another sip. He would usually say 'never saw him again *after that*,' four anomalies within this retelling of the story.

"Well that certainly sounds like Dwaine from the encounter that informs my opinion of him," said Nuru. Gwendoline frowned.

"Dwaine's a smart man, I'll give him credit for that, but he's awfully . . . eccentric." Jerry took a drink from his unsettlingly dark beverage and settled into the booth ready to hear their Dwaine story. "So you guys see the inside of the Industrial Centre? He actually have a wood-fired pizza oven out there?"

"Yes and yes, respectively," said Nuru. "I shouldn't have put mushrooms on my pizza: they didn't mesh as well as I thought they would with the rest of the ingredients."

Gwendoline picked up on Nuru's hesitancy to tell the full Dwaine encounter so she jumped in before Jerry could exclaim about Dwaine's pizza oven. "It looks like it's constantly set up to be able to feed a small group of people."

"Word on the street is that he hosts, or used to host, gatherings of some of his friends and they'd all have pizza. I haven't heard anything about any gatherings out there lately, but I bet he's just a man who needs to be always on the ready for a pizza party . . . for some fucked-up reason."

"It sure didn't look like there's been anyone out there in a while," said Gwendoline. "Does he still come into town?"

Jerry lifted up his head and put his hand under it, exhaling loudly. "I think he still comes into town. He must. I don't know where else he would get his food and other essentials." Jerry's eyes started floating around the room. It was odd that he'd never actually seen Dwaine since the incident. "What's he up to out there?"

"He's working on some old truck, fabricating a bunch of parts from scratch outta carbon fiber. It's pretty neat."

"Anything nefarious going on out there? He's not making a bomb or something like that is he?"

"He doesn't seem to have locks on any of the Industrial Centre doors," said Gwendoline, deciding the hand would remain undisclosed.

"Now that's impressive." Jerry smiled and took a big drink. It was off-putting how much he was able to drink considering how stuffy and not-dry the tavern was. He was growing more and more punchy and Gwendoline decided that if they didn't leave within the next two minutes, they'd be there for the next two hours. "Ugh." She looked at the clock hanging over the bar. "I know we just got here but we gotta take off."

"You sure you can't join us for a round of Go Fish?" said Jerry, even though the moment Gwendoline had looked at the clock Jerry had instinctively started getting the cards back out expecting them to leave.

"I don't know if I know how to play," said Nuru.

"Well it's not that complicated, but we do play it with a little twist!"

"Maybe the next time when we find ourselves in here again we can play," said Gwendoline. At this point she didn't care that this polite departure banter formality was coming off rather heavy handed.

"We can get a game of Yahtzee going if you've played that before."

"No, that game gives me hives." She slammed the rest of her bourbon and they stood up.

Bartender Sarah saw them and stopped knitting. "Oh no, you guys aren't already going are you? You need to come back tomorrow for margarita night!"

"We'll see what we can do, but don't keep the light on for us!" said Gwendoline. Her tone sounded put-on. "We're just two young busy people in a world full of things designed to keep two young busy people occupied!"

With that, they said goodbye to the regulars and stepped outside, waving to Sarah all the way out the door. They pointed toward the livingspace.

"Well that was somewhat entertaining," said Gwendoline.

"You sure were subtle about getting us out of there in a respectful manner." He looked around letting his eyes adjust to the outdoors, silhouettes of red and blue houses burning into his vision.

"Sometimes I just don't think it matters. They seemed

drunk enough to where I could have explicitly told them to fuck off and they'd still invite us to play cards."

"Sure." He nodded but wasn't sure if that was true. "They have a high tolerance though."

"Maybe."

"But did we learn anything truly new there? It seems like things were just confirmed with how crazy Dwaine is. I'm more convinced that he's wild enough to cut off someone's hand, but I don't think he did it."

"He seems to be a rather passionate person." She kicked a dirt clod.

"You think we can take the old way back? I'm getting homesick for our old route."

"Sure, that's fine with me."

"I wanna get a little sinkhole action in me, do some decompression."

CHAPTER ELEVEN

The one-handed mayor emerged from his house for a walk with Louis and looked at the sky. It was objectively how it always was but today the one-handed mayor saw it as more pretty than he had the day before. Louis led the way this afternoon and that meant the route with the most smells. Presently, Louis neared the smelly sinkhole and noticed two people, presumably also there to smell things. The smaller one was standing near the rim of the sinkhole and the larger one was sitting near the bottom. These people occupying space in this area excited Louis and he bounded down to greet the one within the sinkhole.

"Oh! Who do we have here?" said Nuru as the dog

scurried up to him and started licking his pants. Nuru liked dogs and was always delighted to meet a new one. He checked the tag on the dog's collar and the dog started licking his hand, tail wagging hard. "Why hello Louis, how are you doing today?" Louis was surprised that the man knew his name and liked the man very much because of it. However, for as much as he liked him, Louis couldn't stay long since he had yet to greet the one standing on the other side of the sinkhole.

Gwendoline overheard Louis's name and when he'd scrambled up the other side of the hole, she immediately said, "Louis, sit!"

Louis was taken aback but sat obediently—not wanting things to start off on the wrong paw—and was rewarded with pats on the head.

"Oh you're such a good dog, you are," said Gwendoline. She smiled and Louis was both pleased and satisfied with the positive feedback. Gwendoline looked up and saw a man, presumably the owner of the dog, walking over. He was older and looked as if he'd been chronically emaciated for a long period of time before very recently returning to a normal weight. He was wearing a brown jacket and thin wool pants with many straggler fibers backlit by the sun. His face was wrinkly and he had a unique and somewhat exaggerated gait.

"I see you've already trained Louis—thank you for that—I've been meaning to teach him commands for a while now." When in public, the one-handed mayor was able to seem like a normal person, but for some reason, near Gwendoline he felt that he didn't have to force a level of authenticity. He could see just by looking at the way she smiled that she was a genuine person, the type who could see through efforts of one trying to emulate someone they are not.

"It was my pleasure, he's a very smart dog and has been a joy to train." Gwendoline felt a pleasant feeling as she talked with the fellow dog person, and man who clearly didn't get drunk playing Go Fish at the bar every Thursday.

"In all seriousness though," he said, "I was actually out searching for the two of you. I noticed you hadn't walked past my house in a while so I was using my search and rescue dog to track you down. It looked like it worked."

"Ha, yes." Gwendoline squatted down and started patting Louis, thanking him for his service. "We switched up our route recently but I can assure you that we're safe." Nuru had climbed out of his washing machine chair by this point and joined them at the top of the sinkhole.

"Hi, I'm Nuru," he said addressing the one-handed mayor. Nuru brushed his hands against his pants which had come in contact with dirt as he climbed out of the sinkhole before extending one to the mayor.

"Oh! I'm Gwendoline!"

"It is a pleasure to meet the two of you. As I said," addressing Nuru, "I've seen you walking past my house many times and at some community events, I think. My name is Anik."

"Good to meet you," said Gwendoline. She didn't like shaking hands.

"How old is Louis?" asked Nuru. "He seems awfully chipper."

Anik looked at the dog. "He's around six years old. Must be that chipper due to a midlife crisis."

"Indeed," said Nuru.

The two didn't know what to say next and there was

a period of silence as everyone stared at the dog. Louis relished the attention. Just when he thought he'd been acclimated to pats on the head, Gwendoline would switch up her technique and Louis's tail would start wagging profusely again. She eventually had a thought pop into her head that resumed communication.

"What community events do you know us from? I can't remember the last community event I was even at."

"I'm sure you can remember the event once I say what it is," said Anik. He smiled in sly happiness. "It was the pancake toss. You were both there and came in third which entitled you to a small amount of rare syrup. It was an underwhelming prize."

"How the heck do you remember that?" asked Nuru. He was astounded that this guy seemed to know so much about them and Nuru'd never even registered his face. However, the moment the words came out of Nuru's mouth, he realized that he did know Anik from somewhere. "Oh wait a minute, you're the mayor! Glenred!"

"Yes, that's me," he replied, somewhat discouraged to be associated with his profession. That's how it always was for him.

"I'm sorry I didn't recognize you. People always call you by your last name or say 'the mayor' and I think the only time I've heard your first name spoken, I thought they were saying something else." Nuru looked down at Louis but soon got over himself. "We just were at the tavern and talked to Jerry whom you probably know."

"Yes, I know Jerry." It seemed there was truly nothing Anik could do to escape his position when outside his home. Even the out-of-touch young people knew who he was.

"He and Sarah seemed to be throwin' 'em back," Nuru continued. "Both in good spirits today." He paused. Silence filled the group again as they all looked at Louis.

"Say," said Gwendoline, "as mayor you must know just as much community lore as Jerry does—probably more, you're probably more sober than he is too—what's your take on Dwaine out at the Industrial Centre?"

"Why do you ask?" Anik hadn't thought about Dwaine in a long time and was visibly amused that these two young people were interested in him. "You loitering around the FDC super late at night and ran into him?" Anik felt a spark inside his chest ignite a fire, which began to thaw his frozen insides. There is nothing that gets a person more riled up than talking about a person who is constantly riled up.

"Is that when he comes into town?"

"Unless he's stopped. He acquired keys to the place and goes there every once in a while. I was informed about it but he's not going in to vandalize or poop on the floor so I just sent a thing to the Centre telling him to make sure he remembers to lock it when he leaves."

"You know there're no locks on the Industrial Centre doors," said Nuru.

Anik looked at him and then looked at Louis. "I didn't but that does not come as a shock. You've been out there I take it? Does he still have his pizza oven in there?"

"Yes to both," said Nuru.

"Also not surprising."

There was another period of silence.

Gwendoline stood up from her squat leaving Louis alone on the ground. "So, pertaining to the lore of Dwaine, I'm sure you can add to our repertoire . . ."

"I could probably talk to you all day about Dwaine but it would be mostly tales similar to what Jerry told you. Dwaine's run-ins with me are like Jerry's except I've had more of them. He's an enthusiastic fellow who cares deeply about things that others probably shouldn't care very much about."

Gwendoline frowned and squatted again, giving her some time to think (and pet Louis). The idea of introducing the severed hand into discussion was ping-ponging around in Gwendoline's brain and had reached a volume which she could no longer stand. The mayor was technically the highest ranking official in the community, but she didn't want to risk the rumor spreading further. Anik, because of this, however, was probably the best bet they had in learning more about Dwaine's hand in the hand.

"So what was your own personal opinion on Dwaine using other people's cash for personal projects and annexes at the Industrial Centre?" Gwendoline asked.

"Overall I didn't really mind. It's a tactic as old as time and he was taking resources from people who had too many. However, I didn't appreciate that he was using our own workers for those projects. If he wants to get a bunch of raw materials shipped in from some flooded city, that's fine with me—just don't use our community's labor to install it. Do it yourself. That's my official position." Anik squatted down too, patting his knees to get Louis's attention. Louis, fickle when it came to pats on the head, noticed and hopped over to check in with his trusty companion, allegiance to Gwendoline gone for now.

The mayor's nuanced take on local labor didn't get Gwendoline any further to her goal, but at least now Gwendoline saw that the mayor didn't seem like the type of person who'd gossip. They didn't take the direct approach with Jerry and it didn't help anything. She stood up again. "I ask because he gave us a tour of one of these so-called vanity project areas and we found a severed hand in it and we're trying to figure out who it belonged to."

"Oh," said the one-handed mayor, "it belonged to me."

CHAPTER TWELVE

Internally, Gwendoline and Nuru's jaws dropped so low that they were almost touching the imaginary ground. Externally, they just watched the mayor continue to pat Louis on the head. Anik picked up on their masked expressions, "I have a prosthetic hand." He lifted up his arm perpendicular to the ground and rolled up his sleeve. He pointed with his real hand at a small flesh-toned dot near the underside of his wrist. "This button is the only evidence that I have a mechanical hand so I forgive you if you didn't notice. Most people don't."

This raised more questions in the two that both never previously thought of, mainly because both never thought they'd get this far. In truth, Gwendoline fully expected the tavern to be the extent of their search. She squatted down and Louis's damp breaths against her cheek made her recover enough for a follow up question to appear in her mind. "And how did it end up down there? If you don't mind me asking."

"That is a long story that I don't know if I have the energy to tell," said Anik. A slanted expression denoting pain briefly crossed his face. However, his heart changed the moment he took a new breath. Something inside him seemed to be pushing the idea that it would be optimal for him to tell his story—a story that he'd told no one else. Repressing the story had not caused his body pain—it was benign within him—but his body was telling him *now is the time to cut it from my chest and flush it down the drain.* "No, I think I actually do have the energy, if this is something you two are interested in hearing." He waved at the dog, stealing Louis's attention from Gwendoline.

"Yes of course we are," said Nuru.

"How about I drop Louis off at my house and we go to Café B? I'd invite you to my house, but there is only one extra chair."

"That works for me," said Gwendoline. Nuru shook his head in the affirmative.

"Alright Louis, let's start heading back home."

Louis was sad at the mention of home since it seemed to him that they'd only just begun their walk. But as the two new people walked alongside his companion on the walk back, his mood picked up again. He walked over to smell a brick caked in dirt before scampering back to sniff and/or lick the hands of his newfound friends. Louis was very sad when they arrived back at his home only to find that his companion and the two others were continuing on a walk. Sad, but also happy for his companion to get in more exercise and smells.

The group arrived at Café B and found it empty, as it normally was. The building was one of the few in the community that had a higher glass-to-siding ratio, made possible by its line of picture windows breaking the building into two half cubes separated by transparency. Due to its disuse and its continuous air filtration system, the inside was immaculate. Nuru ran to the restroom while the others prepped their beverages. Anik punched in an order for yarrow tea and Gwendoline got hot water, adding a couple scoops of decaf instant coffee from a container that was sitting out. She tried to avoid caffeine in the afternoons. The two sat down and soon Nuru reappeared, getting some water. The sterile interior may not have been the best place to tell a story so far from clean, but in the mayor's mind there was no other option. He took a sip of tea hoping that yarrow really did have medicinal properties.

CHAPTER THIRTEEN

Anik's Story

"I've been in many unfortunate places in my life. I think I always get through them. I'll get through this one. This one isn't even nearly as tragic as this one, the one I'm about to tell you two." He shifted in his chair and put one leg over the other. "Must have been about seventeen years ago now, maybe closer to eighteen, when these events started to unfold. As I was saying, I was in an unfortunate place then. I was living with a woman whom I didn't love. I think I maybe loved her at some point, maybe it was born from convenience. Convenient love maybe. We lived here, in a different place in town than where I'm at now, closer to the center. A blue house instead of a red house. We were living together and there came a point when we both realized that we needed to be apart. If you know anything about 'real life,' you know that 'just separating' is not as easy as it sounds. I should mention that even though both of us realized we should be apart, neither of us said that to each other. In fewer words, we were together, but not together. I figured out that she'd started seeing someone else but I didn't care. The fact of the matter is, finding out she was giving handjobs to another man motivated me to pursue a relationship with someone who'd reciprocate feelings of— capital L—love's deep emotional attachment. That's who I was looking for. The first time I saw her was at an event I put together—I've been mayor for too long—well, that was the first time I *saw* her, but not the first time I interacted with her. I wanted to do an event similar to curling, but make it more fun, themed for our community. I called down to the Industrial Centre to see if they could make some curling stones out of diamond for the event. I talked to a chipper man over the phone whom you two know. He said that he could 'for sure' do that and that he'd put me in touch with someone there who he was planning on hawking the project off to. So I started text-based communication with Darcy. We got the details of the curling stones all fleshed out. Anyway, this is boring and nothing relevant happened from our text chats. I digress. I invited her to the event and promised her and her team free drinks—a tongue in cheek gesture that only old people understand—since I wanted to get people from all sects of the community to the event and the recluses out there would be a nice addition. I'll never forget when I saw her because my jaw actually dropped and a bit of barbeque jackfruit slipped out of my mouth and discolored my shirt. I was shocked at how beautiful she was. She was like someone I didn't think existed outside of my head. I knew that she had to have been the one I was in communication with—at that point I probably knew about fifty percent of everyone in the community

and *no* community member is that attractive. I remember
it like it was yesterday. It was like my brain told me to take
a picture of this exact instant of time and remember it
for eternity. She was wearing a mustard colored sweater
with blue jeans. She had straight, dark brown hair that
went down just below her shoulders. She was wearing yellow sneakers that matched her sweater and the sneakers
had blue stripes on them. Her face was a formal study of
beauty for artists of the high renaissance. She was talking
with two other people I did not recognize, but correctly
assumed were from the Industrial Centre. All three of
them were sharing a plate of mini sandwiches shaped like
curling stones. There were even little handles made from
tiny pieces of carrot on the top of the buns. I walked over
and introduced myself as the mayor and thanked them
for helping make the event possible. As I looked at her up
close, I felt something tickle my insides: it was like some
sort of little love fairy was me giving me courage to try and
butter her up. The love fairy ultimately might have been
galvanizing my insides to withstand the stupid remark I
was going to say next, maybe it was the save-face fairy.
I tried very hard to block out what I said to them but I
still remember it almost verbatim. It was something like
'are you all enjoying the curling stone sliders? They really
slide into your mouth, too bad you can't pick them up by
the handle though . . .' Just, just what a dumb thing to say.
But by the grace of God they all seemed to get a kick out
of it. Next, I went for the jugular and made an inside joke
with her relating to our prior correspondence. You know,
in order to cue her in that we had a connection a little
deeper than the two she was with. Recalling this, I wonder
if I was shooting myself in the foot, but I think if I had said

anything else, things would've still worked out how they did. At this time, I was too blind to see that she took an interest in me. In hindsight I could tell, but that's how that is. She had brown eyes that had a hint of yellow in them, her eyes were looking at me and she had a slight smile on her face. Probably amused at my lame remark. What a face she had. I looked at her face and could see beauty and intellect and a pure conscience, and other things that I may have wrongly projected onto her. As I was saying, I couldn't initially read her. I talked with the three of them for a while and from that inferred she was not in a romantic relationship. We got on a subject that neither of the guys she was with were interested in and they took off to eat some more sandwiches and get drunk. We talked about all sorts of unimportant things, we talked about how silly it was that all the houses here are either red or blue—me strategically leaving out my own opinion on that—and we talked about all of the events I'd spearheaded. She especially liked hearing about the cotton candy themed soccer match we did. I don't know what motivated me to actually pursue doing a cotton candy themed soccer match. Maybe it was just the fact that it was a bad idea. I remember she got a kick out of me saying that the winners of the match got to eat as much cotton candy as they wanted, but the winners ate very little cotton candy because the cotton candy I'd made tasted really bad. We talked about what she did at the Industrial Centre. It sounded like a bunch of boring stuff but she assured me that it was exciting, at least while the Centre was being built. She invited me out to the Centre and I invited her to another upcoming event. After an hour or so of talking, I was even more in love with her than I was when I first saw her. Our next meetup was at the Industrial Centre, probably our first official 'date.' I was up front with her and told her that publicly I had a romantic partner, but there was no longer an emotional connection between us. She was fine with that. I only later told her about how I found out about my partner's infidelity. Sorry if I'm getting too adultish for you guys, by the way. It's just another love story." The one-handed mayor laughed. His voice sounded worn, like his medicinal tea was starting to eat away at his throat.

"We kept things on the down-low for the sake of my job or reputation or something. In hindsight, there was no need for me to want to keep things secret. I was just too much of an effing dummy to end the old relationship. It's hard. You'll find that out, I hope. I've learned from my mistakes now anyway, I think." He took another breath and looked out the window.

"So we would see each other as much as possible. We'd go walking all over the place, I co-opted her onto the city council and various other bureaucratic-type groups. We had our inside jokes, we had pretty much everything we wanted. Life was like a montage. Whenever I had a bad spell, she'd coax me out of it. Whenever she had a bad spell, which was never, I would've helped her out of it. In general we just helped each other out. She was working on a play. Her childhood dream was to become a playwright but she was too smart for that. So romantic sounding, but it was just a hobby. I helped her create a universe in which the characters interacted with one another and the universe interacted with the characters. Forgive me, I'm getting lost in more romantic talk. I thought I hadn't ever used my imagination before meeting her. She introduced me to a world outside our own, with its own characters and its own events. You can scoff all you want, but it was magical."

His eyes snapped back to the interior of the café and sipped his tea.

"The story from here takes a turn I'm sure you saw coming. The montage ended. The music stopped. Things slow down and soon the story ends. Again, I'm sorry if you two young people think this is a load of 'crud' or what have you. The fact of the matter is, this is just me recalling my life." He took another sip and looked outside again. "We were romantically engaged for about a year and a half when I noticed a slight lack of energy from her. When I look back, I think I remember the exact moment, but I think my mind could be rationalizing and tricking me into thinking I knew the exact moment. The day came when she didn't feel like doing anything—not a hike, not a swim, not think of characters for some story or another, just nothing. The inferior being that I was, I thought that I had done something to anger her, but she assured me I hadn't. It took some convincing on her part because I was skeptical that I had overstepped my welcome in some way or another. It wasn't me though. We started seeing each other less and less. I had no idea what was going on. Her excuses were vague and I became worried. After about a week of not seeing her, I went over to her house and let myself in. She was lying on the couch and was happy to see me. She reassured me that it was nothing that I'd done; I'd understood by then that she was ill. She felt bad and dropped the secretive act. She told me that she was sick and she didn't know with what. She said that in the past she'd been experiencing some troubling symptoms. She was steadily getting weaker and weaker. She was losing muscle mass.

She started losing bits of her hair. This is where things get difficult. I was trying to figure out what she had, doing research, et cetera. I'm sure you could guess in a second what she had. It would take willful ignorance to not realize that she had radiation poisoning. I arrived at that conclusion before she did. Well, I should say that I proposed that before she did. I bet that she knew what it was right away. How couldn't she have? I think that if you know what you have, and you know that you're going to die from it, and the death is going to be painful, then it's only natural for you to deny your death. She refused to believe that she'd been exposed to radiation at the Industrial Centre. She said that there was no way that could be the case, that she always wore protective gear and that the machines didn't ever break down. She said that no one else was working on anything radioactive. There were a few possible solutions: I think the one I prefer is that she was getting doses of radiation over a long period of time which was slowly damaging her body. I was doing everything I could. She was practicality vacuuming up stem cells. Bone marrow transplants. We—meaning mostly I—were treating her as if she had radiation sickness. Nothing was working. She was throwing up blood, her brain started not functioning properly, She started treating herself with alternative medicine. She started to pray all the time. She would pray to the gods of all the religions. She started burning candles and did acupuncture—honestly those aren't the worst, I respect those. I didn't like the smell of the candles. They smelled like dried wood mixed with melted plastic. They didn't work. When she admitted they didn't work, she started looking into spells and magic and stuff of that ilk. She was weak. She'd lost all her muscle mass, had very little fat. Her eyes no longer had any intensity. I'm probably wrong but at the time I thought that the bit of yellow she had in her eyes had faded to brown. She would speak some gibberish that was some ancient language or what have you. The day came when she asked me for my hand. At first I thought she wanted us to get married, to experience her few last days or weeks of life in a formal relationship built upon love. What she was actually asking was for my actual hand. She wanted to sacrifice the hand of a lover to save her life. What would you do if someone asked you to cut off your hand for them? You'd probably call them crazy. I mean hell, I thought I'd be the one to call that crazy. That's not what happened. There was nothing I wished for harder in my life than to trade places with her. She didn't deserve to die the way she did. She and I were so dissimilar. I was always the one who used the phrase 'kill me' in a less than ironic tone. She was the one who always wanted to live. So I mean what the fuck? What did I have to lose? I'll cut off my hand if it means it would make her happy. Am I crazy? I mean shit, I don't know, I guess I am. I cut off my hand so she could perform a spell with it? Honestly I didn't ask about what the spell was. I didn't want to know. I knew she was close to death, I just wanted her to be happy. We went to the cistern and I cut off my hand and she said some words. We left the cistern and she died five days later. It should've been me." His eyes snapped from the window to his cup of tea.

"I'm so sorry," said Gwendoline.

"There's nothing I can say," Nuru added.

"Don't worry about it, guys. I'm fine. I've recovered to my normal self. I went through a dark period, but I'm back living in the gray. Also, you two are both young. You will experience heartbreak and tragedy. Everyone does. It's not about how bad the event is. It's about how you handle it. You will experience deep pain. You'll experience thoughts that tear down the image of the self you've spent so long constructing. You'll experience hatred and fear. All of those things. I can only say that it's easier to go into them if you know that it is just that—fear. There's nothing you can do about some things. I don't know where I'm going with this. Just know that when you have a painful experience, know that there is more pain than good in the world, and when you acknowledge this, the amount of pain within you decreases." He lifted the cup to his lips and let a tiny amount of tea into his system. "Decreases a little." He nudged the cup away from him. "You have any questions?"

"Um, not really. I'm sort of still taking this in," said Nuru.

"I tacked on a moral to the end of my story and I want you to know that most of the time it's hard to remember that there is more pain than good. I've spent most of my life in pain. Maybe pain is too strong a word: maybe emotional limbo, the lack of pain, the lack of feelings. Maybe that's what I've been experiencing. But at the same time, there's nothing and no one who can change my physiology. Knowing this, the only thing to do is to learn who you are. That may help you. I don't know if you need this information, I'm blabbering at this point. It's cathartic. Anyway, my story is similar to just about everyone's who's ever existed on this planet in one way or another. You guys are making me want a beer . . . I don't want a beer." Anik took a sip of tea and this time could feel its medicinal effects. He was feeling the opposite of what his conscious mind told him he would feel. Instead of feeling sad, he was feeling the touch of catharsis on his shoulder, its warm feeling seeping through him.

Gwendoline was ready to ask questions. "So you never figured out how she died?" Nuru glanced at her with a look of masked disgust.

"Well, I know *how* she died. But, correct, I personally never knew what exposed her to radiation. I think she may've known or may not. I've always leaned towards the first."

"But she never gave you any specifics?"

"Correct." He paused, giving Gwendoline time to think. "I've discovered closure. There was no foul play involved apart from her working in a dangerous field for the majority of her life."

The one-handed mayor had tricked himself into believing that, but knew his period of comfortable belief wouldn't last forever. In his heart, in his subconscious, he'd tucked away the thought that Darcy was too adept to let something terrible happen to herself. He did not, however, try in the slightest to suggest that his closure had an expiration date. It was a subject that he didn't like thinking about, even if it no longer had the same sting as it used to.

"I'm glad you were able to move past it," said Nuru. "It can't be easy."

"Well, again, I'll be honest with you, it's not. Now the hard thing is continuing to report to my position every weekday where I sit and do nothing."

"Well it could be worse," said Nuru, spinning his empty water cup, "you could be doing something."

"When you get to my age a lot of time it *is* better to do nothing than something sometimes, but I can tell you, it's a lot better to do something than to do nothing." He frowned and looked out the window. Maybe the medicinal effects of his tea were exaggerated. "That being said, there is an event coming up that you guys may be interested in. I've had a lot of people request this and I've always thought it was too dumb, but it's finally happening. The community is doing a lawn bowling tournament but instead of lawn bowling it's on sand and uses beach balls. Beach bowling. I told them it wasn't going to work and suggested medicine balls and a gymnastics floor—as a practical alternative—but people are very keen on having it beach themed."

"We can sure try and make it," said Nuru. He was a tad intrigued but Gwendoline wasn't. It could be an opportunity to learn more about the mayor, but the event probably wouldn't be ideal for it.

Anik looked at his watch. "It's getting late and I managed to make myself hungry with all this talking. I think I'm going to get over to the FDC tonight and pick up something special, being that it's Thursday and I've met two interesting members of our community."

"We don't want to keep you from starving," said Nuru. He caught himself speaking like his father and frowned internally.

"And thank you for that," said Anik, getting up and neatly pushing in his chair. The other two got up to say goodbye and parted ways. Anik was in a cheerful mood as he walked to the FDC. He couldn't remember the last time he'd felt this cheerful. A weight had been lifted from his shoulders. He never knew just how much that incident was weighing on him until it was lifted off. When he arrived at the FDC, the attendant was surprised to see him and even more surprised when he picked two pieces of fish—along with his usual jar of peanut butter.

CHAPTER FOURTEEN

Gwendoline broke their *no-talking-on-the-way-back* etiquette only moments after leaving Café B. "I can't help but get this feeling there was something shady going on with Darcy's death."

"Oh God, here we go. You think so?" Nuru pressed his lips together as they walked and exhaled through his nose. He'd had thoughts of the same nature too but wasn't the type to pursue them out of respect for Anik.

"I don't like that they never figured out what caused her sickness."

"It must've been something she'd worked on in the past or something there that was leaking radiation."

"No, I don't believe that. I think you'd start feeling sick right after being exposed. I don't think there's such a thing as chronic exposure. Your body can be exposed to radiation for long periods of time—given that it isn't too strong—and your body will fix your DNA. I'm thinking that she got exposed at the Industrial Centre. There must have been something there that was causing radiation."

"There was no way that was the case. Didn't the mayor say that Darcy said it couldn't have been there?"

"Do you know where we can get a Geiger counter here?"

"Oh no." Nuru vibed Gwendoline had gotten something lodged into her head that wasn't going to leave until she'd uncovered and isolated all possible variables. The remainder of their walk was spent in silence.

It was about dinner time when they arrived at the livingspace and Nuru headed straight for the fridge. Gwendoline plopped on the couch and thought more about what the mayor said. "You think they rent out Geiger counters at Fire & Equipment?" she asked, half jokingly in order to ease Nuru into her real question.

"Hell no, no normal person needs a Geiger counter. We'd have to go to the Industrial Centre and steal one from Dwaine," said Nuru, picking out a dense bread containing dried fruit from the fridge. He had a suspicion where she was going but made no attempt to let it appear so. "And I don't think we're going to be able to do that. He's probably already suspicious that we're going to try and figure out whose hand it is. He's probably figured it out too."

"Wouldn't your dad know where we could get a Geiger counter?" Gwendoline tried to hold back a smirk.

"Goddammit," Nuru felt his heart sink. "Do we really need a Geiger counter? I don't understand why we need a Geiger counter."

"We need the Geiger counter to find out if Darcy was receiving doses of radiation. Obviously she didn't think it happened at the Industrial Centre so why not her house? I bet they didn't do any scanning or whatever there."

"Well how do we know that for certain?"

"The only places where it would likely be happening on a continual basis are at her home or while she was traveling from her home to the Industrial Centre. Therefore it would make the most sense that she was receiving radiation at her home."

"Or at the Industrial Centre and they never actually checked, I guess." Nuru wasn't looking forward to visiting his parents' house, especially to ask his dad for a favor, but he wanted to humor Gwendoline.

"But what happens if we find the source of the radiation? What does it prove? It proves that either someone was deliberately poisoning her or the ground under her house was radioactive. Someone could've known and there could be a cover up, or maybe no one knew and never looked into it. I mean, yes, it does make the most sense to assume that she got radiation poisoning from something she was working on at the Industrial Centre or before her time there, but I mean let's take a look at the facts: most radiation poisoning isn't going to be *that* delayed."

"You don't know that." Nuru sat and started eating the bread.

"Well in any case Dwaine or both could've killed Darcy and I personally would like to figure out how she actually received radiation poisoning."

"We don't even know that Darcy is a real person," said Nuru in his final hurrah at convincing Gwendoline that they did not need to take a trip to his parents' house.

"Oh, come on. You don't have anything else going on and your parents are super nice."

"Fine, we will go to my parents' house and I will ask my father if he can get us a Geiger counter. This is going to be a big waste of time when we don't find anything radioactive at her house—that is, if we can find her house—and if word gets around that we were trying to pin murder of the mayor's secret lover onto a community member . . ."

"That's the spirit!" said Gwendoline, suddenly standing up. "I haven't seen your parents in a dog's age, probably not since you last saw them."

"Well fuckin' A, they're nicer to you than they are to me."

Gwendoline realized she was standing and hopped to the fridge. "We gotta keep this on the DL because I'm sure the mayor suspected we were going to prod further and there's no doubt in my mind that Dwaine is going to try and figure out whose hand it is too. He probably had some vial in his pocket and got a skin sample or some shit when we weren't looking and did a DNA test cross referencing it to community records that he somehow has access to."

"You're already in too far." He pinched up a bit of crumbs that had spilled onto the floor and placed them on the coffee table.

"Well that could be an exaggeration, but it seems that's as plausible as anything else."

"This is gonna get us killed or some shit."

"No it's not. The only way you can get killed is at your parents' house. We're essentially doing the hardest part—for you—first!"

Nuru finished his bread and started mentally preparing for his parents. Gwendoline found nothing satisfactory in the fridge so hopped onto her personal computer to check the Archive for Geiger counter operation, unsympathetic to Nuru's familial woes.

CHAPTER FIFTEEN

Dwaine had been stewing over the hand ever since they found it, still wondering how to proceed. He had not, in fact, obtained a DNA sample from the hand and therefore had not cross-checked it with any DNA database. He did, however, have access to one. That would've done him no good anyway. He'd only gotten as far as knowing that the hand must have come from someone Darcy was associated with; however, he did not know anyone still living who fit that description. He barely knew anyone with whom she associated when she *was* alive. Dwaine looked at the concrete cube array in his warehouse. He was punching himself in the metaphorical gut for not knowing more about Darcy's personal life, but that information was never that important to him. He still didn't know how to proceed. There were too many open-ended questions for him to stay inactive, but even for a person as intelligent as himself, he was at a loss. The only thing he could do was spy on the two but that seemed rather petty, an activity a paranoid person would do. He decided he wouldn't spy on them and got back to working on his truck but quickly changed his mind after installing the last tire pressure gauge. He decided he'd rig up a telescoping surveillance camera on top of a spire, nothing too crazy just yet. He still didn't know why he was worried anyway: he had nothing to fear, he didn't cut off the hand.

CHAPTER SIXTEEN

By the next day, Nuru had gathered enough mental energy to visit his parents. The two went around noon, hoping to catch his father in a good mood relaxing after finishing lunch. The house looked like all the other blue houses in the community except it was the only one that had an ornamental orb, among other decorative items, in the front "yard." Nuru's mother was heavily invested in lawn ornaments, even if no one in the community had more than a gravel driveway.

"Do we knock?" asked Nuru.

"You're not that much of a stranger, are you?" she said, hoping he wouldn't knock so it would potentially startle his parents.

"I think I should probably knock."

After some bumping inside the house, Nuru's father met them in the doorway. "My son! My golden boy! He hath returned!" Nuru's dad was even taller than Nuru and built like a tank. When younger, he had an athletic physique but as he aged it morphed into one of a retired powerlifter who never gave up his maximum performance diet. "You're no stranger here, you know, you could've let yourself in!"

"Nuru was very clear that he didn't want to startle you in case you were napping." Gwendoline loved Nuru's dad but did find it understandable that Nuru didn't like coming home. One can only handle being the butt of jokes for so long.

"Such a kind and thoughtful man my son has grown into, living all on his own. But why has he returned? There can only be one reason." He waved them into the house.

"Oh you know we just swung by to say hello and check up on you," said Gwendoline before Nuru had time to respond.

"That really warms my heart, it truly does." He grinned and pointed at the couch.

"This is totally you, Gwendoline," said Nuru. "We're here because of your plan, not mine."

"I knew it, Gwendoline wanted to reunite the two of us and rekindle our family spirits!" He lifted his hands in the air and gave Nuru a hug before his son was able to sit. "Take your shoes off first for pity's sake!"

They made it to the living room and Nuru's dad took a seat in *his* chair.

"Where's mom at?"

"She's out doing one thing or another. Gathering food for the two of us, after our son left, leaving us to fend for ourselves."

"How cruel he was for that," said Gwendoline.

"She'll be back around sixteen hours. I know you're going to be too busy to stay till then, so I'll tell her you stopped by and that you send her your love."

"Thanks."

"So what brings you back home?"

"We—read: Gwendoline—need to get a Geiger counter."

Nuru's dad looked up through the ceiling into the sky, "God, I look up to you. Have I failed in raising my child? Have I succeeded? What does it mean when your first born returns home asking if I can get him a Geiger counter?"

"I'd say you've succeeded," said Gwendoline.

"You come into my home—which used to be yours, which you left—three and a half weeks before your mother's birthday asking if I can get you a Geiger counter." Nuru's dad was working himself up into a manic state. "What can I say to that?"

"Gwendoline is the one who wants the Geiger counter, not me." Nuru was trying his best to not break and give his father the satisfaction he was looking for.

"Well, in that case," his father quickly regaining composure and looking over to Gwendoline, "I think I could get one." His eyes flicked back at Nuru and he shook his head. "Three and a half weeks before your mother's birthday . . ."

"What does that even mean?" said Nuru. "How does that relate at all to this?"

"You'll understand when you're older." He shifted his weight in the chair to address Gwendoline with his full attention. "What I'm thinking I'll do is have Nuru's loving mother run it over to you tomorrow when you're at home so she doesn't feel bad that she missed you." He shifted his weight and crossed his leg, now addressing Nuru, "Or, you could come back tomorrow and see her."

"Also when you get it, can you make sure to keep it on the DL?" said Gwendoline. "We're going to be doing some covert operations with it that'll require one to be discreet."

Nuru's dad made a strange shape with his mouth. "I'll see how discreet I can be when taking a Geiger counter, but I can't promise you that I won't tell someone that I'm borrowing it," he said in a rare earnest voice. "I'll have to let the big boys know that one'll be missing for a day. Not that anyone's used 'em in the past twenty years."

"Well just make sure you don't tell them that you're taking it so your son can break into a house and search for radioactive material," said Gwendoline.

Any earnestness present in Nuru's dad's voice was now gone, "I have failed as a parent! Lying to my contemporaries so my son can get away with criminal mischief! How far the mighty fall!" He was back in an agitated state.

"I don't know what to say, he's fallen in with the wrong crowd. It just happens," said Gwendoline, pushing Nuru's dad further.

"They always start with Geiger counters. Soon that isn't enough and they move to X-ray equipment. Then and suddenly"—Nuru's dad snapped his fingers—"boom, vintage uranium-refining machines. It's a slippery slope, Nuru. This is your warning . . ."

"He may be on the wrong course now," said Gwendoline,

"but his heart is still in the right place." She paused and imitated an owl by rotating her head as smoothly as she could to look directly into Nuru's eyes. "But as they say, the road to hell is paved with good intentions."

"Amen!" Nuru's dad clapped and jumped out of his chair. "It's important to remember that, my son." He sat back down and grinned.

"Well, we should really be going, I have to water my plants," said Nuru, in a truly sad attempt to become the one spouting patronizing remarks.

"You're good, I watered those this morning before you woke up," said Gwendoline. She looked at Nuru and noticed cheek muscles bulging from his face as he pressed his tongue onto the roof of his mouth as hard as he could. "But actually I think I missed that cactus on the sill."

"Yes, thank you," he said to Gwendoline. "I knew there was something you'd missed."

Nuru's dad shook his head, "My son and his wonderful friend are leaving already, here one minute and gone the next." The three stood up prompted by Nuru and he slowly herded them to the door. "Before you leave," Nuru's dad's voice now somber, "make sure you don't press the self-destruct button on the Geiger-counter."

They started their walk to the livingspace and right as Nuru was starting to relax, his dad yelled, "Hey, you want some ham loaf? We got a lot of ham loaf!"

"I'll pass!" He couldn't help himself and turned around to figure out if his father was joking or serious. His father looked serious and Nuru took a couple brisk steps before returning to a normal pace.

CHAPTER SEVENTEEN

It was the next day and Dwaine had just finished installing a surveillance camera on top of one of the diamonds. Whether it was fate or whether it was just luck that this had happened at this time, Dwaine didn't know, but he acknowledged that this was an interesting time for him to be going out of town for two days. On one hand, he knew if he were here, he'd end up wasting a lot of his time looking at the camera live feed, but on the other hand they could discover something important while he was gone. But on the *other* other hand, he thought it may be good to get his mind back onto something he had a positive passion about: Scientific Instrument Transporter Spotting. For the past two years he'd planned to go down south and watch the heart of the newest, and soon to be largest, fusion reactor in the world travel to its final destination. Dwaine had watched all the major fusion reactor convoys, almost all the giant telescope convoys (the ones since his 30s), and many odds and ends like hyper colliders, warp drives (all had ended in disaster), and various instruments bound for space. He wasn't going to break this trend for two detective kids' roleplay, if that was even happening. Plus, if they did anything he needed to know about, he'd be alerted.

Dwaine watched a little bit of the live feed and felt disgusted with himself. "Ah fuck." He waved at the screen dismissing it and went to pack for his trip. He needed to leave later that day and regrettably placed setting up the surveillance camera higher than packing on his list of priorities. "God I'm such a fuckin' paranoid prick," he said under his breath as he walked over to a brown metal cabinet housing his clothes. "Fuckin' A." He got clothes for the next two days packed, went down a couple levels to a place not disclosed to Gwendoline and Nuru, and quickly ran through the aircraft checklist. He brought it up to the main level and got it outside, carefully following the paths for the wheels he'd cleared. As he took off, his uneasiness lifted from him as the plane rose into the sky. The other Sci-Spotting crew he'd run into down there was now at the forefront of his mind. It would be mere hours until he could chastise Bill about his old glasses. His thoughts about the Industrial Centre were a thing of the past.

CHAPTER EIGHTEEN

Moments before Dwaine finished installing his surveillance camera, Nuru's mom had started her walk home after dropping off the Geiger counter. Nuru's dad had stayed true to his word and let no one know he'd taken equipment.

"It was nice to see your mom," said Gwendoline.

"Yeah, she's much better at being a normal person and not giving me constant shit."

"Well that's one way to say it." She sat on the floor and opened the Geiger counter box. "I guess now once and for all we can find out if bananas are radioactive."

"Oh God, please." Nuru turned off his personal computer and spun around in his chair. "You really don't have to fill the role of my father."

Gwendoline put on her best taken aback face, "No one could ever do that!" She turned on the machine and held it up to a banana. "This doesn't seem to be working." She looked at the side of the unit, adjusted a knob, and reapplied it to the banana. The machine made a loud beeping noise, startling Nuru. "It seems to be working."

"I just wanna say this now. You really do not need to go around testing every object in this place. Nothing's going to be radioactive."

"That's the problem. You don't see things how I see them. We can't be sure everything in this room isn't radioactive unless we test every object." She looked at Nuru with her brows raised and froze briefly for effect before returning the Geiger counter to its box. "Now we just have to figure out where Darcy lived."

Nuru looked up at the ceiling trying to think. "Obviously we could go to City Hall and look through the records. That would be annoying and people would know who we are. We could do that from your computer too but people would also know who we are."

"I'm wondering if that would set off any red flags. But is anyone actually looking at the logs of who looked up certain information on X day? Seems like we could find out right before we plan on going. What, is the webmaster going to report us to the mayor in five minutes? Actually now just saying that, I guess I could see that as logical, but I don't think that would be something that actually mattered to the dude."

"It's better to be safe than sorry." Nuru fidgeted with his hands. "What I think you should do—because I'm not logging in, you are—is just look up a bunch of other shit too to obfuscate our motivations."

"Is that taking things too far or not? I think if anyone was to check the logs—which I don't think anyone is going to do—they'd see the weird and suspicious thing and think that we just looked at other houses in the area to cover our tracks."

"I don't really know why we're even talking about this. No one is going to check the logs and so what if they did? Is the mayor gonna be like, 'Hey, I am the mayor. Please do not break into my dead lover's house trying to find radiation,' I can't see that happening."

"Ok, so to find out where Darcy lived we just look it up. Check. How do we actually get into the house and how do we do it without being spotted?" said Gwendoline, thinking out loud but open to Nuru's input.

"What I'm thinking is that we learn how to pick locks."

"You've got to be kidding me."

"Then we throw down a couple smoke grenades."

"Genius." She sat down at her personal computer. "What if the doors aren't even locked like at the Industrial Centre and we can just walk in?"

"That sounds like one of my dumbass thoughts," said Nuru with a thin smile.

"Dwaine obviously has security up the asshole there so it doesn't matter if the doors aren't locked, but I don't know."

"What I'm thinking is easiest is if we just show up wearing some retroreflective vests and go in through the window on a ladder." He'd started the thought as a joke but it ended up sounding feasible by the time the words left his mouth.

"Well we can't go under the cover of darkness until the winter so that doesn't actually sound like half bad a plan."

"Well yeah, I mean I see people in those yellow vests all the time. Let's be real, if someone came to the door in one of those vests and a ladder under their arm and told me they needed to do some work in the bathroom, I'd be like 'yeah go for it.'"

"But then how do we acquire a couple of those vests and also how do we make sure that the neighbors don't recognize who we are?"

"Those are questions I think you should answer," he shook his head, bouncing the burden to Gwendoline.

"We wear masks."

"I like where this is going," said Nuru and grinned.

"And *then* we go in."

"Alright, I'll get out the paper and washable markers and we'll get to work."

"What if I didn't go and it was just you?"

"Oh come on," he groaned and dug into his chair.

"If people recognize you, they'll just think you finally were getting out of the house and making yourself useful. People already know that I'm never going to do that."

"Well what would you do while I'm doing that? And we don't even know where to get a retroreflective vest anyway."

"Your dad can get us one or two I bet."

"You can't be fucking serious. Why didn't we think of this earlier? I really, really don't want to go back there." Nuru sank into sadness at the thought.

"How about this, I pretend to be a guy and we go in together."

"I don't think this plan is gonna work."

"I don't think that people would even give us a second thought if we were to go in just dressed as we normally are."

"I think you're right. So why would we even need to get vests?"

"What we need to do is cover all the bases." She stood up and put one foot on her chair. "This is about sliding over home plate without losing our lives."

Nuru frowned. "So when are we going in?"

"Right as soon as you tell your dad that we need two retroreflective safety vests."

"Wait, so we *are* still doing that? I don't think we need to do that."

"It would be in our best interest to make sure we stay covert. We should also bring our ladder with us as well." She continued after a moment, "What about this: I talk to your dad and ask for two vests and see if he can leave them at some neutral drop point. That way you don't have to talk to him again and we can wear vests."

"Whatever, do what you need to do." Nuru got up to enter his sleeping area to get away from Gwendoline's harebrained ideas. It wasn't that he was skeptical of her theory, but he was skeptical of them needing to be covert. What harm would it do if neighbors saw them going into the house? But Gwendoline's mind was in plan mode and there was nothing that could stop her now. He went onto the Archive from his PC_X to see if he could find some lock picking tutorials.

As Nuru hid, Gwendoline shifted gears. She sent a message to Nuru's dad, who responded nearly instantly informing her he had a bunch of vests at the house and they could come at any point and get them. She hopped on her Personal Computer and logged into the city archive, finding Darcy's info in about three seconds. She looked over the Transaction, Maintenance, and Fund History and frowned.

"Yo, Nuru get your butt over here and read this."

Nuru looked up from his screen exhaling loudly after only a minute of solitude. "I'm watching a video on how to lock pick, what is it?"

"This TMFH is frickin' sus as shit."

"What about it?"

"Just come over here and look," Nuru exhaled again, louder this time. He got up and looked over Gwendoline's shoulder. "It says here that the house was closed after she died and then it sat there vacant—I'm guessing since it's a shitty house and there are better houses that people could move into—until the city put it up for some rejuvenation thing or whatever 'Community Urban Revamp' is supposed to mean. Then like eight months later they canceled the project and it's still sitting vacant to this day."

"Oh shit, are you thinking what I'm thinking?" asked Nuru, knowing Gwendoline had been thinking what he was thinking before he was thinking it.

"If you're thinking about being excited to go and see your dad in a half hour to pick up those vests, then yes."

"Goddammit, are you kidding?" He groaned and impulsively squatted down on the ground.

"No I'm not, but *also* this is the same house that Jerry was talking about." Gwendoline started grinning and her eyes grew bright as she started constructing her new conspiracy theory. "Dwaine had to kill Darcy, no question about it. Think about it, he has a grudge on Darcy or something that we don't know about because it happened before we knew about all this shit. He fucking passively tortures her to death giving her doses of radiation in her house—why that way? Could be symbolic of something, some competition they had, I don't know—and knew that the house would sit vacant. Then when it's announced that they're going to knock it down or let someone else knock it down, he jumps on it because there's still freaking radioactive material in the ground and/or furniture from where she was being poisoned. He makes up some cover story about some worker—or I guess that's real—he intentionally reignites some conflict that he had with an Industrial Centre construction worker to get people—the *right* people—to think that he's building an ice cream place to spy on that person or whatever. Then when the project fails, he can be justifiably angry anyway. Then he tries to block all other projects on the space and eventually the city council gives it up. Maybe even the mayor thought the rejuvenation project could be a way to low-key commemorate Darcy's house and when it backfired, he pulled the plug."

"Shit, sounds plausible." He mulled over the new information while looking up at the ceiling. He spotted the shape of a duck in the plywood. "Would he really want to let people know that he was building a place just to spy on a worker? You'd think he'd keep that under wraps since there's no suspicion of him being the one who killed Darcy anyway. How would it be suspicious at all that he wanted to build a place there?"

"You know, I guess what could've happened was just poor luck that sorta worked out in his favor? Like, he didn't get to build a place on the land and clean up the radiation, et cetera, but going forward, everyone would think that he just wanted to build the place there because he was spying on some worker. In that case it's bad luck for him but also somewhat convenient bad luck."

"Hmm, that seems like it makes sense, but what if we don't find any radiation at the house?"

Gwendoline stood up from her Personal Computer and looked out the window. "We will find radiation at that house, I have no doubt in my mind."

CHAPTER NINETEEN

"Alright let's pick up these vests and break into this house." Gwendoline started putting on her shoes.

"Wait we're doing this today? It's like the middle of the day!"

"Yeah we're doing this today, when else would we do it? Is there a benefit to waiting until tomorrow?"

"The benefit of not having to see my dad two days in a row," said Nuru as he sulked over to the shoe mat.

"Your dad probably isn't even going to be home. It'll just be your mom if your father is to be believed."

"Well that makes me feel slightly better about the whole thing. Do we actually know how we're going to get into the house? There's no way we're gonna be able to get in through the doors. They probably have some heavy duty locks on that shit for people like us." They stepped outside, heading toward Nuru's parents' house. "Also, how are we supposed to not look suspicious if we're entering the house from the window?"

"All we do is put the Geiger counter all around the sides of the house making it look like we're checking stuff. Then we just scan the windows and pop out the glass to check the seams of the window. Easy."

"Yeah whatever." He shrugged. "At least it's a nice day out."

Gwendoline looked around and agreed with Nuru's

assessment of the weather. "I feel like we haven't been able to have a good walking conversation during this whole severed-hand fiasco."

"What are you thinking about now?"

"Well I don't know, most of my thoughts have been hand-related. My thoughts about the philosophy of art and thoughts about nu-consciousness have gone by the wayside."

"I guess that's what happens when you've got something going on."

"Yeah I s'pose so." Gwendoline looked at the red and blue houses and went silent for a tad. "What do you think we'll do once this is over? I don't think we'll ever find a severed hand again. I've derived a lot of motivation from this and I'm worried that going back to being a stupid forgettable artist is going to be less fulfilling."

"Eh, I don't know about that," said Nuru, who unlike Gwendoline, actually had no activity he could fall back on to pretend he could no longer like. "I think you'll just continue to make art stuff and if it no longer interests you then you'll stop."

"Seems fine." She looked for a clod of dirt to kick but there wasn't one near her.

"I think there are events that break up our lively rituals that can impact us negatively, positively, or neutrally, and this fiasco could be any of those. If we figure out that Dwaine killed Darcy, what will that have changed in your own life, or mine for that matter?"

"Yeah, good point. Maybe this is just a technique at self-procrastination for putting off creating new shit."

"That's an interesting thought, especially since this whole thing started by you working toward your next painting goal. Seems like you're just being falsely apprehensive about your future as some sort of unconscious humble brag, since I'm clearly the one with less of a future."

"That's an interesting thought," said Gwendoline, grinning. She'd never thought of her thoughts that way, propelled by her ego. Maybe it was true and perhaps she was full of courage and always would be. She was skeptical and afraid of that thought. "I think in any case it's good to be wary to some degree as long as you're still moving forward. Something like having low expectations but extremely lofty sights. That way you can smash through your expectations and have a mentally easier time reaching your goals. Maybe one expectation is that when this is all over, I go back to living a boring life where I live in our virtually post-scarcity world constructing self-portraits of my feelings. There's something lame about that, but also empowering, I guess."

"Well I don't know. Seems to me like most people could do your weird self-indulgent shit," said Nuru, slightly trying to provoke Gwendoline, "but they don't because they aren't comfortable with themselves or lack the skill or motivation to try and get the skill, for whatever reason."

"I don't know where we're going with this conversation anymore but it seems to be headed back to a *young person in a big world* trope, which I guess is relevant to us even if it's cliché or whatever." Gwendoline briefly looked over at Nuru and her cheek twitched as she imagined herself at age sixty, depressed with no energy.

"I think it's honestly much shittier for me," said Nuru looking up at the sky, "I've essentially been dicking around—not that that's a bad thing to do—but I fear that all the dicking will bite me in the ass on my deathbed. I'll be old and look back at my life and say all this time spent dicking around looking up shit on the Archive was a big waste of time. Maybe this post-severed hand incident will serve as a way to knock me out of that rut."

"Maybe, but I doubt it. I just wonder to what degree you'll be able to, based on how our community is set up."

"Oh here we go again," said Nuru, grinning as he saw how eager Gwendoline was to bring politics to the conversation.

"I'm just saying that even if your mind comes into the right place of wanting to pursue something or break through the rut, you may not have the social capital or resources from the community to do so. We're slightly different being so isolated up here, but it still stands in any size city. Being an artist or a writer is easy—I got lucky that way—there's virtually no overhead and you don't *need* a community to do it. But if you wanted to become a physicist—and I'm not saying that you would want to, I'm just saying some person in general—you would need a lot of equipment to test all their shit that you just can't find anywhere."

"Yeah, I get that element, so you're essentially telling me that even if I break out of the rut that I'm in, and I don't think that it's even productive to call what I'm in a rut—it's all how you think about it to some extent too—but I still could be fucked over. What a message of hope."

She kicked a dirt clod. "That's what I'm here for. But, who knows, you could have other callings or get some less expensive hobby or go down south and put in some hours doing hard labor for free. At the end of the day—or when you're on your deathbed—I don't think it's going to matter what you've done in your life. I think it's going to matter more how you felt on a day-to-day basis and if you were trying to discover some key to some lock."

"Yeah I don't know if I completely agree with that, but I don't think that's necessarily wrong either. People just live different lives and maybe that life for both of us is solving an unsolved murder, which maybe isn't an unsolved murder because no one besides us—you—thinks it was a murder. We just go back to coasting however we coast. For me, that's wasting my life reading a bunch of dross about high-powered pogo sticks, and for you that's making a bunch of shitty art that helps you learn more about yourself even though you already know about yourself."

"Maybe."

"And I'm not trying to be cynical about that, I'm just saying some people like me get off on learning about high-powered pogo sticks."

"The fear lies in your case—that I see at least—in not ever applying your knowledge to anything productive. You're essentially falling into some sort of hedonism for trivia nerds."

"Yeah I guess in some ways I am just taking up space, but I'm also not really harming anything besides the multitude of people who find me insufferable." Nuru blinked twice and felt puzzled.

"We'll both end up like Jerry anyway, telling his favorite story about something outlandish that happened once. Living in the past, only looking at moments we remember. Our lives ultimately won't be different than any other successful or unsuccessful person. We'll just have stories we can tell at the tavern or concert hall to appeal to whoever is gathered around us. I don't know. I just worry that my life is going to peak and then it'll go to shit," said Gwendoline. She looked at Nuru who was again staring off into the sky.

"With that attitude it probably will!" He snapped back into reality.

"Maybe what I'm worried about is that I won't have any takeaways from my experience. I probably will, but they'll probably take a while to manifest in my mind . . . and I'll probably keep on living in relative ease and not unhappiness."

"I can tell you a couple takeaways right now," said Nuru. "Breaking into a building and then pretending to be a city employee is bad form and will make people mad at us."

"They won't be mad when we catch a murderer."

"I don't know, they very well could be angry. We could have this whole thing wrong too. There could be multiple people involved, we could've been lied to by Jerry. There're a ton of other possibilities. She could've just gotten sick. Even if we find some radiation trace, she could've just put it there herself. Too many possibilities. Plus, what if Dwaine did kill her? Do we frickin' tell Anik? He'll probably sink into some inescapable state."

"He didn't seem to be doing that bad when we saw him last."

"Well is that for us to decide? He told us that he had let it go and was at peace with her death."

"I don't know if I completely buy that shit."

"Well I'm just saying that it might not be for us to decide."

"I don't know where you're going with this, but we're going to break into an abandoned house this afternoon and we're gonna find radiation and perhaps some way to tie it to Dwaine."

"Yeah, I'm sure we are. And some neighbor will spot us and ask the mayor or Jerry what they've planned for the building and they'll be confused and then the neighbor will tell them that they saw two people who told them that they were doing some surveying work for an undisclosed project. That could set Anik back into something and we'd be total assholes who lied to him. We both saw that he looked better after he was done telling the story."

"I'm not trying to shit on him when I say this, but people like him are always going to have ups and downs like that. I think it'll bring him *true* closure when we isolate the last variable."

Nuru exhaled through his nose and choose not to respond.

A while later they arrived at Nuru's parents' house. This time Nuru made a point to walk in without knocking but neither parent was home. "Huh, I guess they just left the door open for us."

"That would agree with what this note says," said Gwendoline, who'd walked over to the vests flopped over a chair near the door.

"Does it say where my mom went?"

"Yeah, looks like she had to flee from the secret police before they could arrest her for helping two young adults break into an abandoned house."

"Damn." He looked down at the floor and crossed his hand over his chest, "God help her."

"No, she took off to go help your dad with some shit, it looks like."

"Ah, that's good to hear that she hasn't been captured."

"They're building a gazebo together apparently and they're wiring it up today."

"I wonder where they're putting it." Nuru rubbed his face and yawned. "Seems like there isn't too much space on the property for something like that."

"I agree but knowing your mother that won't stop her from filling up their whole plot with crap."

"I don't know, I feel like maybe a gazebo serves a purpose, especially if it's got lights and heat and stuff. Good place to hang and look at your lawn ornaments."

Gwendoline picked up the vests. "So when do we put these on? We should probably put them on now and walk over there right? No sense in putting them on just as we arrive."

"I think we put them in a bag and put them on a block before we hit the place."

"Also we forgot to bring the ladder with us, you think we should go back and pick it up?"

"I don't fucking know, do we actually need a ladder to get into the house? I don't want to walk across town again carrying a ladder especially if we don't need it. If you feel the need to bring a ladder, just take the one my parents have. We have to come back here anyway to bring back the vests and the Geiger counter."

"I don't want to get you in trouble with your parents," said Gwendoline, grinning.

"Yes, thank you for looking out for me. I appreciate it. I'm just saying that I don't think we're going to need to use a ladder to get into the house."

"Well maybe, but what I'm thinking is that it'll add to our credibility with the neighbors."

"I'm not gonna carry the ladder, you're carrying the ladder." Nuru went deeper into the house to fish out a ladder.

"Shake my damn head, Nuru. It's like you want us to get caught," Gwendoline said as he disappeared.

A moment later, Nuru was back with a ladder under his arm, a screwdriver, and a piece of chalk. Gwendoline eyed the chalk and a devilish grin appeared on her face. "Now I *know* you're thinking what I'm thinking with the chalk."

"Hell yeah I am," said Nuru, now grinning since Gwendoline was grinning. "Slap down some Xs and arrows on the ground or on the foundation of the house. People will be like, 'Damn, these guys must be taking some measurements of something.' No one's gonna bother us if we put some random chalk marks down on the ground."

"Absolutely genius." Gwendoline grabbed the ladder from Nuru. "I'll even carry this thing after that epic thought. Wow, this is really light."

"Yeah, much lighter than I remembered it being, that's for sure."

"Alright, so we have the ladder, we have some chalk, we have the Geiger counter, we have a screwdriver. Is there anything else we need? Right now it seems like we don't have anything that will actually help us get into the house."

Nuru cocked his head to the side and turned around into a different room. A moment later he emerged with a cordless reciprocating saw. "This should do the trick."

"What the hell we gonna do with that? Take out a fuckin' wall?"

"Yes."

CHAPTER TWENTY

With full hands the two departed, starting the walk to Darcy's house. It was about a fifteen-minute walk and

Gwendoline was itching to resume conversation in the same vein as the one they had earlier. "So hypothetically, what you're saying is that I'm taking too much of a utilitarian approach to my life?" she said, referencing her perceived difference in opinion with Nuru on whether experience needed to be cultivated from life and always applied to future actions.

"I wouldn't say that, but I think there's something to be said about not constantly analyzing one's life. No point in doing that too much. Once in a while is fine and necessary, but not all the time."

"Well there's probably a way to integrate events and allow them to better one's decisions going forward."

Nuru looked over at Gwendoline and then a cloud, shaking his head. "I think what you're describing is called learning."

She laughed. "Damn, I guess you're right. I guess learning is important." She shifted the ladder from one hand to the other, forcing Nuru to walk into the ditch as the ladder swung. "But then how do we learn to learn?"

"I don't fuckin' know, Gwendoline," he said in a short laugh, "look it up in the Archive?"

"I forgot where I was going with this anyway. I think I'm just getting that feeling I get of being a young person who doesn't want to waste their life but thinks that I'm going to inevitably waste it."

"Well, luckily you can only waste your life if you think you've wasted your life." Nuru didn't know if he believed that to be true, but there was no harm in putting up a counterargument.

"I guess. It just seems like I'm going to make a bunch of crap and then die and that'll be the end. I'll have made a bunch of crap. I guess you're right in that making a bunch of crap isn't any more virtuous as not making a bunch of crap."

"I mean, I guess you could probably extrapolate that from what I said . . ."

Gwendoline shifted the ladder from one arm to the other again. "What I still don't understand is just how open-ended everything is. There is no crisis for our generation to solve, a luxury but also a curse. Our generation collectively has no post-severed hand mystery to keep them occupied as previous generations have had. Everything has been solved and all that we have left are science experiments and art."

"Eh, I think we have more than that, but I do understand the bittersweet situation we're placed in. You're also speaking more for this community rather than the world at large. But yes, the generation forced to be trapped in their own minds because we don't need to have our attention deviated elsewhere. Then we look for something else to arbitrarily focus on, like make up a conspiracy theory," he said, without intention to provoke.

"I think it's a feeling that can sorta make me feel empty inside on some nights. Some nights I feel as if I'm imploding but I'm not imploding because I feel that I don't even have a body. Then other times I feel as if I'm surrounded by people who care about me and care about what I'm doing and that feeling doesn't exist. I don't know, life's just too open-ended and I have no doctrine to follow because I refuse to follow one that someone else wrote but I'm too unmotivated to write my own, not to mention the lack of faith I'd have in it if I did write one of my own."

"Don't they say all that shit comes in time? Like, by the time you're in your sixties you'll have made your own doctrine to follow and it'll be very similar to everyone else's doctrine, but who cares, you're old."

"Yeah, I guess that may end up happening. Who knows though, such trivial thoughts. Such privileged thoughts that I'm allowed to focus on. The feeling of obligation when there are no obligations. Too much open-endedness. It's hurting me."

Nuru smiled. "Well you can take solace knowing that there were a bunch of smart people whom rich people paid to solve problems, which were never solved, nor can be solved. The only conclusion the smart people came to is that you can't solve them. At least not with words, or words in the way we know them."

"Fuckin' bullshit, all of it. Like all this science shit is going to help us come to some understanding about who we are." Gwendoline was half-angry and a little melancholy at this point, not knowing how to proceed with the conversation. A period of silence took hold and the two admired the beautiful day.

After a couple minutes Gwendoline's mind reengaged, wanting to finalize their plan of attack. "So what I'm thinking is that we check the door right away. See if it's unlocked. There's a chance that it could be. After that, we go around to the windows and see if they're unlocked. All the while we're using the Geiger counter and making random chalk marks. Then, if we can't get in through the windows, we use the ladder to get up onto the roof and see if there's a skylight or a vent. It could be there's just a vent we can open and go right in. All we'd probably have to do is unscrew some screws. They could be riveted down, but in that case we bust out the saw and either saw the vent open or saw through the roof."

"I think we're going to hit insulation unless we use the saw strategically. A vent could be good if there is one, I was thinking that maybe around the window frame could be good too. That way we could take out the whole window, get some pictures, and measure it so people would think we're replacing the windows."

"Bulletproof." Gwendoline grinned a little. Her heart was beating faster the closer they drew to the house. Nuru, on the other hand, was not getting excited. He was in a neutral state. Realistically, he knew no one would care if they were at the house, but was still minorly worried that word would reach the mayor and open old wounds. In Nuru's opinion, that outweighed the need for Gwendoline to figure out if parts of the house were radioactive. However, he was excited to break into a house, something that he'd always wanted to do.

About a block away they stopped to don their retro-reflective vests. "How do I look?" said Nuru.

"High-vis AF."

"You know how much I care about safety. I care just about as much as I care about streetwear—a lot. Combining the two isn't easy, but it can be done. I'm proof."

Moments later they arrived at the abandoned house. It was two stories tall and looked like two painted blocks stacked up on top of each other with the top block three quarters the size of the bottom and pushed to the back. It was a red house with two windows on either side of the front door. On the corner of the roof perched a weather vane in the shape of a rooster that disrupted the building's otherwise perfect symmetry. The metal siding went all the way down to the ground, as if one day the house had sunk in order to escape the anxiety of an animal taking refuge underneath. Without saying anything to Nuru, Gwendoline walked up, set the ladder down against the wall, and tried the door. It was locked. She looked over at Nuru and pretended to write something down in an invisible notebook, nodding her head in affirmation of an undisclosed something. Nuru set the Geiger counter box near the door.

Gwendoline spoke loudly channeling the spirit of a partially deaf warehouse foreman, "Should we do a perimeter check?"

Nuru looked at her with his lips scrunched together as he fidgeted with the reciprocal saw. "I don't think we need to be fooling anyone here."

"Yeah, Dustin." She kicked the house as hard as she could, ignoring him. "You just wanna go and mark up that front step as clear?" Nuru's eyes rolled as he got the chalk out of his pocket to draw an arrow on the step.

"I forgot that you shouldn't put chalk in your pockets, goddammit."

Luckily, Nuru's wound-tightness unraveled after he drew the arrow and he relaxed. Something about drawing with chalk must be therapeutic.

"Yep that looks pretty good, Dustin. You just wanna go ahead and get out the black box and fire her up?"

"Sure thing, boss. Looks like we're gonna need to let the bitch warm up for a couple minutes before use."

"Ehhhhhh." Gwendoline entered deeper into her character, making her voice scratchy and jaded. "I've used that fuck right away and it hasn't ever done me any trouble. Just turn it to fuckin' *On*."

Since Nuru had spent most of his time watching

lockpicking videos, he didn't know how to actually use the Geiger counter and left it up to Gwendoline. She slowly circled the whole building at its base, putting the probe right up to the house. The counter stayed silent. "Looks like we're clear to proceed with the windows," she said, still in her foreman voice. The windows were just high enough to where it would've been possible for Nuru to open them while standing, but only a crack. He propped the ladder to the left window and tried to look inside. The reflections in the window were strong and all he could see were the houses on the other side of the street, making him develop a pit in his stomach. Spies. This house was near the edge of the community and only three houses were nearby, each spread a hundred yards from another. Nuru tried to tell if there were any faces peering out from the windows. They looked empty, but that's how all the houses looked when it was day. He let the paranoid thought go and cupped his hands to look through the glass.

The interior looked like every other community house. The living room had an ugly couch, an ugly coffee table, and a stove. The air circulation system was still working and made the room look inhabited—no thin layer of dust, yet no sign of life. He tried the window but it was stuck. It appeared to be locked, and paint on the trim was spilled over onto the window informing him that the window was not meant to open. The other window was the same. "I don't think these are opening," he said in his normal voice, not directing his speech to anyone in particular.

"Yeah well I guess we'll just have to check the others on the sides and back. Eh fuck," she said, still in foreman mode. They checked the remainder of the windows on the ground floor and found them all to be locked and sealed.

Under each window with the chalk, Nuru arbitrarily drew an X, O, or an arrow. They found that the only way to get onto the roof, and second floor roof, was by way of the front of the house. Gwendoline was now out of foreman mode and into problem-solving mode. Their ladder wasn't tall enough to get them to the very top, but she formulated they could pick the ladder up behind them after ascending to the roof of the first floor's landing area. "Well this is going to be interesting." She moved the ladder to the house. "What I'm thinking is that if we can't get into the house from the first floor's roof, we're gonna have to pick this up and take it with us. Then hope to God that there's a way into the house from the top."

"If worse comes to worst, we can probably get the ladder back down to the ground firmly. We'd have to be really careful to not have it tip over when we go down and potentially injure one of us or leave us stranded."

"That's not on the agenda today, just make sure you bring the saw up." The ladder was just tall enough to get them to the landing and Nuru picked it up behind him after finding no way to enter the house except a small, six-inch diameter chimney stub. He let the ladder drag on the side of the house as he slid it up. It made an unpleasant sound, as if the ladder were a bow playing a string that didn't want to be played.

"Well this is probably suspicious," said Gwendoline. "Up we go!" The ladder wobbled thanks to heavy warping of the roof's tar-like sealant material as they climbed again. When they got to the second floor's roof, Nuru realized they forgot to use the Geiger counter on the prior level and didn't bring it up: priorities had shifted to breaking in.

The second story roof was like the one below but with

more surface area. Like the lower, it was covered in a black tar-based coating. Gwendoline scanned the rooster-shaped weather vane but the Geiger counter remained quiet. "Damn, I was really hoping this was gonna be it." On her way back from the vane, she noticed a bracket-shaped seam in the sealant near the center of the roof.

"Yo check this shit out, looks like there's a hatch."

"Daaamn, do all houses have these? I feel like being able to go out onto your roof and chill in a lawn chair is something that every house should have."

"I don't know, our building certainly doesn't."

He knelt down and tried to open the hatch by digging his fingernails into the sealant. It didn't budge. "Well, here we are. On a roof."

Gwendoline was getting antsy and put the Geiger counter up to the hatch. The machine made a faint noise.

"Cripes!" Her heart rate picked up. "Get the fucking saw fired up and let's cut the latch and open this fucker up!" Nuru stuck the blade into the middle part of the seam and started the saw. Within seconds he felt resistance give way.

"Alright, I think we're in." His heart was starting to race too. "What if there's still a lot of radiation down there?"

"Who gives a shit, let's check this shit out." Gwendoline flung the hatch open so fast that it hit the roof and bounced closed. "Take two." She opened the door, slowly this time, and allowed it to rest on the folds of sealant that had caused it to snap back shut.

They peered into a room appearing to function as a storage space. Below them were variable sized crates, a fake Christmas tree, a stack of firewood, and a lot of technologically advanced looking scientific equipment. "Oh shit there's no ladder," said Nuru.

"I guess we're gonna have to jump down and hope to God we can get out. I think it would be smart to throw the saw down first in case we do get stuck." She paused for a second to run everything over before they jumped. "Oh shit, also goddammit what do we do about the ladder? If we leave through the front door, it'll be trapped on top of the roof. Wait, we could use it to climb down here. No, it's not gonna fit actually."

"What if we flipped the ladder around upside down and put the small end in first?" Nuru was half joking but half-serious. "That way we could get down most of the way and the ladder would be safely wedged."

"Then we could get the ladder stuck in the hatch, good thinking."

Gwendoline squatted down and threw the ladder off the side of the roof.

Nuru exhaled and ran his hand through his hair. "My father is gonna ask questions about why there's a bend in the ladder now. You're answering to that."

"Alright, you go down first and I'll throw you the saw and Geiger counter," she said, packing up the Geiger counter and saw.

"Makin' me go down first, eh? Pretty typical behavior there." He gave Gwendoline some side-eye and lowered himself down as far as he could, letting himself fall the rest of the way. "Daaamn, it's neat in here."

"Catch this shit." She threw down the tools and Nuru stepped aside for her descent. She lowered herself making sure that the hatch would close behind her, flipping it halfway up and letting it rest on her head. She landed in total darkness.

"Hold on, I'm gonna turn on a light," said Nuru.

Gwendoline's knees hurt from the jump and she took a step to where she'd remembered seeing a sturdy looking, sittable box. However, the box wasn't where she remembered, causing her to trip and fall. She felt her body fall through the darkness and break through pieces of wood that splintered into her back.

"Goddammit, you could've waited like five seconds and I would've had a light on," said Nuru, flicking on his PC_X light. "Are you okay?"

"Yeah, I think so." She looked at herself and noticed that her right arm was leaking blood. "It doesn't feel like I've broken any bones." She started to get up and looked for a place to put her hands. "Oh fuck oh fuck oh fuck oh fuck oh fuck!" She awkwardly lurched away from the crate, managing to get herself standing. Its contents of small, marble-sized ceramic capsules that Gwendoline recognized as spent nuclear fuel had partially spilled onto the floor.

"Grab that shit and get outta here!" she said, looking frantically for a door nearby.

Nuru spun around, finding one behind him. "Oh shit, over this way." He put his PC_X in his mouth and picked up their equipment, kicking over the stack of empty boxes blocking the door. He shouldered the door but it didn't move. He dropped the tools, stepped back, and ran shoulder first into the door. It flew open and he sailed into the hallway. Gwendoline followed, picking up the Geiger counter and reciprocal saw on her way out. Nuru had dropped into the hallway hurting his ankle as the attic door was elevated about two feet off the ground.

"You okay?" said Gwendoline. "We gotta get the shit outta Dodge right fuckin' now." She tucked the saw under her arm to help Nuru up and the two moved as quickly as they could to the outdoors.

"Well I guess there was radiation up there after all," said Nuru."Let's hope you didn't crack any of those fucking pellet things. This goddamn house could burn down. I'll be fine I think."

"I think I'm more worried about dying an excruciating death within hours at this point."

"In all honesty, it doesn't really make the splinters all over your hands and arms look too bad knowing you've got radiation poisoning too."

"Yeah good point." She surveyed her arms again and started picking out the larger splinters that had lodged in her skin. She could feel the splinters in her back now too.

Nuru sat on the steps. "I'm not trying to be a downer here, but this would be one case where I hope this house has lead paint."

"Fuck off, you weren't the one who fell into that shit. Also I could die at any second." She looked around. Outside was the same as it was when they entered, still fairly sunny, dry air, no one peering through the windows. With her wits now gathered, she started unpacking the Geiger counter from its case.

"Well I guess I should know how much radiation I was just exposed to."

"Christ, and we're still going back in." Nuru shook his head, lips pressed together. He'd been as close to the box as Gwendoline, and for a longer period of time, and didn't feel as if he needed to go back. But he calmed down and realized that not knowing their radiation dosage would be a mental death sentence. "Well I guess we gotta find some more clues or whatever the fuck we're doing here. Take some pictures of the crime scene. Get some leads."

CHAPTER TWENTY-ONE

They headed in through the front door and stood in the same living room Nuru had seen from the window. He was startled by the sheer number of beige rugs splashed on the floor, having previously assumed the floor was one piece of carpet.

"No radiation here," said Gwendoline. "Should we just go for the jugular upstairs? I'm kinda ready to find out how much radiation I just got."

"That seems like something we're gonna have to do." He kicked one of the rugs back in place that had been dislodged as they'd fled and followed Gwendoline up the stairs.

The Geiger counter faintly buzzed as soon as Gwendoline made it to the top step. She looked at the readout on the side. "We're fine," she turned around to Nuru, "at least at this distance." She made her way down the hall but stopped in the bathroom doorway. "Dang, nice bathroom to be honest."

Nuru squeezed himself into the doorway. "Wow, this is a nice bathroom."

It was made almost entirely of polished marble with much of the space reserved for the shower. The glass panels enclosing the shower were intricately frosted and etched with a scene of what looked like two intertwined figures dancing. The figures were surrounded by bubbles etched like they were popping out of the glass, giving off a pleasant glint. The toilet was antiquated and extremely heavy. Neither Nuru nor Gwendoline knew how it was supposed to operate. Nuru stepped into the bathroom and a stream of water started pouring into the marble basin from a slit in the wall. He gravitated to the chain hanging from the ceiling. Its links and handle were also made of marble. He pulled it and heard a faint whooshing sound. "No way," said Nuru, opening the lid to the toilet. The water was already completely still. "How is it that this house is a dump everywhere except for this room which looks like something from a medieval king's house?"

"I don't think kings lived in houses."

Nuru's mouth slanted and he watched Gwendoline disappear from the doorway presumably to the attic. She didn't make it that far, instead stepping into the bedroom adjacent to the bathroom. The Geiger counter's readout told her it wasn't *too* unsafe.

"Yooooo," said Gwendoline, noticing a painting of the cistern hanging on the wall. As she approached to get a better look, part of the wall swung open into the bathroom. "What's up?" she said to Nuru as she walked through the hidden door.

"Just checking out the bathroom still, you know. I see you've discovered a hidden door that automatically opens as one draws near. No big deal though, they've had that kind of stuff forever. Check this out." He stood in front of the full body mirror and text appeared in the glass. "Yeah that's right, you can check to see what you have in your fridge from the mirror. Freaking bath and food culture melded together as one."

"What's in the fridge right now?"

"Doesn't look like anything is."

"Oh well that's probably a good thing. How do I get out of the bathroom using the hidden door though?" She looked around and faced where she entered but nothing happened. Panning to the floor, a little circle cut into the marble near her feet came to her attention. She reached down and touched it and the door swung open. "Hmm, I guess we're breaching etiquette by leaving our shoes on in here. Doesn't look like this li'l button was designed for people wearing shoes. This is a big toe button if I've ever seen a big toe button before, which I guess I haven't."

She came back into the bedroom, this time followed by Nuru. It was very plain. The bed had neither sheets nor blankets; the blankets were folded neatly on the chair next to the bed. The closet looked like it was made out of a laminate that resembled wood as much as a leopard covered in mud did. One of its sliding doors was crooked. There were also a large number of rugs on the floor; these rugs were the only thing that took the room from plain to bizarre. Gwendoline stepped closer to the bed and the Geiger counter started making noise.

"Oh goddammit." She looked at the readout and grimaced. "We should probably actually get the hell out of here. It's giving me a bunch of warnings." She backed up and the two left the bedroom. Back in the hallway, Gwendoline looked down at the smashed attic door and rubbed her teeth on her upper lip. "Seems like that fucking shit I fell into is right on the other side of the wall from the bedroom."

"That would make sense."

"Alright let's blow this joint before we get cancer or something." They walked downstairs, peaking briefly into the other rooms. "Do we venture to the basement?"

Nuru's facial expression told Gwendoline that he didn't want to go into the basement, but he spoke anyway. "I'm not sure what would be gained."

"Yeah me neither, I kinda want to get out of here." They left the house, locking the door behind them. Gwendoline looked at the Geiger counter history on the side of the unit as they stood in the sun.

"I'm guessing from what I saw and what this says, we probably were both exposed to around half a Sievert at most. The Geiger counter wasn't reading *too* hot, but still pretty fricking hot. I didn't get close enough to the bed, but it looked like if she was sleeping there, she was exposing herself to maybe one hundred or two hundred millisieverts a night-ish. I don't really know how to calculate that shit, but I think even being so close to it won't be that bad. I am starting to feel a little sick though. Not sure if that's due to me getting radiation poisoning or from me thinking I'm getting it. I think those pellets must've been fairly old."

"I don't know, I feel alright. I don't really know how I should be feeling. Isn't half a Sievert like a lot of fucking radiation?"

"Yeah but I don't think it's enough to kill someone. And that's me being conservative too. That's the high end. We were probably exposed to less. I don't know how many capsules of that radiation shit there actually were either. What did the mayor say again? Something like a month or two that it took her to decline?"

"Yeah something like that. So we were much closer to the radiation than she would've been when sleeping, but she was exposed longer. I don't fucking know. Obviously it was enough to kill her though," said Nuru. He looked around making a note to remember to get the ladder.

"We're in a tough position here now, goddammit." Gwendoline looked around too. Everything was exactly how it was when they went in last time except her eyes felt sunken in. "We have no proof that Dwaine was the one who put that crate up there either. If my exquisite brain is continuing to function properly, the crate said something like 'caliper parts' on it in someone's handwriting that I didn't recognize. I saw Dwaine's handwriting when we were at the Industrial Centre, and that wasn't it."

"Even if it was his handwriting, I don't think that's enough to pin this on him to be honest," said Nuru. He departed for the side of the house and retrieved the ladder. No damage. The only evidence of mistreatment was some dirt clinging to one of the feet, which he wiped off with his thumb.

"So what do we do now?" said Nuru, standing with the ladder under his arm. He picked up the saw, letting Gwendoline carry the Geiger counter.

"I don't know. I need some time to think."

The two started walking back to Nuru's parents' house, and just as luck would have it, a neighbor had taken this time to step outside and survey the plant life growing near his house. Gwendoline and Nuru waved as they walked past the house and he yelled out to them, "What's up with that house? The city planning on finally doing something with it?"

Gwendoline smiled at him. "Not to my knowledge. We drew the short end of the stick on inspecting the place for particulates. Gotta be done every once in a while even though the heat's on and the circulation system is registered as working."

"You find anything? Pretty bold going in without masks . . ."

"Yeah there's some stuff up in the attic that'll need to come out at some point. Hopefully I can wrangle someone else into doing that."

The neighbor smiled. "There was some weird stuff in that house. Not surprised that you found something. Surprised no one's gone and looked in a while."

"Well, my guess is no one annoyed the muckety-mucks enough to where they forced us to go do it!"

The neighbor laughed, "Have a good one you guys, don't piss off too many people. Nothing good ever comes from that, not that I would know!"

Gwendoline gave a chortle and Nuru smiled at the neighbor as he turned away. "Christ," Nuru said, "you could've told me that we were gonna be mold inspectors."

"I didn't know that we were until I said it, but I think that went okay."

"You shouldn't have said the thing about angering the muckety-mucks. I think that increased the odds of our actions being brought up to someone later. Maybe you were too talk-y," said Nuru.

"Whatever, I don't care. If he says anything to anyone, they'll be confused and'll just pin the task on someone else who may have issued it. They'd have to be all together in the same room for us to be found out. Plus, that dude might take our interaction with him to the grave. He looked like the type of guy to do so, if you know what I mean."

"Who knows. I think I'm feeling a little sick now too. Let's reconvene our minds at a later point." The two walked back to his parents' house in silence. As they approached they saw that both of Nuru's parents were home.

Nuru's dad saw them from the window and opened the door right as Nuru was about to twist the handle. "I see you've taken our ladder with you." He noticed the saw in Nuru's other hand and lifted his head up slightly to look through his close-ups. "And our reciprocal saw."

"There was a kitten stuck in a tree so we had to take them. It was the only ethical choice," said Gwendoline. She stepped into the house and took off her vest; they'd both worn them the whole way back.

"Oh I know how that is, sometimes you just gotta be the hero."

"How'd everything go?" said Nuru's mom, appearing in the hallway. She was holding a small unidentifiable electronic object.

"Pretty good," said Nuru, smiling.

"Please tell me you didn't let yourselves get exposed to high doses of radiation."

"You don't have to worry about us," said Gwendoline. Nuru's mom instantly picked up from Gwendoline's non-answer that, indeed, she did have to worry. Any time Gwendoline took over the conversation, it was to keep Nuru from getting trapped in a lie. "We took all necessary safety precautions when making the world's largest banana smoothie."

Nuru's dad popped in again, "If you were making a banana smoothie, wouldn't you wear a color other than bright yellow? Wouldn't you be afraid someone would accidentally throw you into the blender?"

"Good point."

"Well I suppose we should get going," said Nuru, setting everything down in a neat pile. "I don't wanna throw up all over the floor from the radiation poisoning I just received. I can do that in my own home." Even though he said it as sarcastically as he could, it was obvious he was trying to cover his tracks.

"You're free to throw up on this floor whenever you like," his dad said. "But I have no problem with you doing so on your own floor."

As soon as Nuru's father closed the door on them, he got a readout of the Geiger counter's history.

"Oh Christ."

"What's it say?" said Nuru's mom.

"Looks like they were exposed to around half a sievert."

"What! Where did they go?"

"I'm not sure. Had to be somewhere in town. No GPS on this unit."

"Well, I hope they don't die!"

"They shouldn't, but they probably'll get very sick for a bit."

CHAPTER TWENTY-TWO

Back at the livingspace, Gwendoline and Nuru were getting sick. Gwendoline was sitting in front of her personal computer debating if her own sickness was because she was exposed to radiation or because she anticipated events to get hairy with Dwaine. "How do you feel?" she asked Nuru.

He was sitting on the counter after deciding that he couldn't stomach food. "I'm feeling kinda cruddy."

"We're in kind of a bad position here." She glanced at the fridge and looked away. "We didn't get any evidence that proves that Dwaine was the one who put that stuff in the attic. We let someone know that we've been pok-ing around Darcy's house without permission and they could tell someone and it could very easily lead back to the mayor. The mayor could find out and that could plunge him into some sort of state. I don't know. Fuckin', I should've told that guy we had to check all vacant houses. Anik would lose all the trust he had in us—which could've been very little to begin with—but still, we could essen-tially open up a murder case in which there is no way of proving who the killer is."

Nuru made his way to the couch and lay down. For how weak he felt now, he was amazed that he'd been able to hop up onto the counter. "I think we could've foreseen that something like this was gonna happen . . ."

"So the question is, do we tell the mayor and possibly subject him to even more torture? Why should he know? He said he found closure, not that I totally believe that." She frowned.

"Why did he talk to us in the first place if he hadn't moved on though?"

Gwendoline was lost in her own thoughts and ignored him. "So we could go to the mayor and tell him what we found. That could potentially trigger a terrible situation and get him into some form of dysfunction. And plus, what if it is Dwaine? There's no evidence and people maybe wouldn't even believe him if he did confess. There's no legal authority here to detain him. The mayor would just discover that someone was living happily who killed his lover and there was nothing for him to do about it. This is really starting to misalign with my personal philosophy of staying out of other people's business."

"You're usually so good about that too . . ." said Nuru.

His body was telling him to fall asleep. Gwendoline's was too but her mind was too preoccupied to notice.

"We could drop the whole thing right now. Just be done with it. We could be completely wrong. The box could've gotten moved up there as a mistake and it could've been an accident. What the fuck do we do? We're really in this now. If we do nothing, we could have this bite us in the ass at any time."

"I don't really want to think about this right now."

"Well you don't have that luxury, unfortunately." She swiveled to face Nuru. "What if we get Dwaine to confess and we try and use the power of the dialectic to get them to resolve their issues."

"I know how much you believe in conflict mediation, Gwendoline," he said, trying his best to stay awake, "but I don't think that would work with your level of expertise in that area."

"I think you're probably right. You got any ideas?"

"I don't know, I need to wait until I feel better."

"Fine, I guess I'm on my own here." She turned to face her personal computer but felt a rush of lethargy and decided to take a nap too.

CHAPTER TWENTY-THREE

Two days later, Dwaine returned from his Sci-Spotting expedition early in the morning. Immediately after stowing the aircraft, he checked the surveillance camera footage. On his way out, he had a change of heart and decided not to be notified of activity thinking this would allow him to enjoy his time away more thoroughly. Hopefully that was for the best. The first clip the computer flagged as important was the two visiting Nuru's parents' home. Nuru was carrying a box which Dwaine couldn't identify. "I knew this was a waste of time, goddammit," he said out loud. However, the next clip showed them emerge from the home with their hands full and carrying a ladder. He fast-forwarded and saw them arrive at Darcy's house. "Goddammit for real." He moved away from the screen and did a quick pace before returning to the footage. He watched them enter Darcy's house through the roof, come out, and go back in. This was not good. He moved away from the screen again and started walking around the Big Deep Hole. "How in fuck's name did they extrapolate the hand to Darcy's house? Also, fuck, a Geiger counter?" He didn't know how much they knew, but he knew they must have figured out something relating to how Darcy died. "Goddammit, I knew I shoulda set up that fricking camera sooner." He knew that they knew how she died, or at least knew there was a chance of radiation at her house, otherwise they wouldn't have brought the Geiger counter. They had to have figured out whose hand it was. It couldn't have been Darcy's. What would've prompted the counter? Maybe they asked around and found out how she died. Maybe they were just taking necessary precautions? Dwaine walked over to the screen and watched the rest of the footage. Nothing else. "Christ, maybe those fuckers gave themselves radiation poisoning too. I'll have to send in a fuckin' tip and get a welfare check." He shook his head and continued his walk around the hole.

Unfortunately for him, his drive to figure out whose arm the hand belonged to had begun to increase since watching the video footage. He wondered what simple steps he could take to figure out whose hand it was, but there was almost nothing he could do from the Industrial Centre besides mope. He started a walk around the BDH one more time and decided he had nothing to lose by asking the two if they found out whose hand it was. Besides, he hadn't done anything wrong. Being impatient, and on the far side of the hole from his personal computer, he pulled out his PC_X and looked up Gwendoline's contact information. He sent a quick message and decided to do some more laps.

CHAPTER TWENTY-FOUR

Gwendoline and Nuru were sulking in the livingspace. Both felt down after spending the last two days indoors recovering from radiation sickness. They were on their way up now; each new hour felt better than the last. That being said, they still felt like their insides were melting. Gwendoline's personal computer beeped.

"Who's sending you messages at this time of day?" said Nuru, making a hazy joke stemming from neither having any idea as to what time it was. "It's probably my dad checking to see if you're doing ok."

Gwendoline got up from her bed and flipped on her personal computer. Her brows sunk closer to her eyes as she read the message.

"Who is it from?" said Nuru again.

"It's from Dwaine." She paused to cough. Swallowing the disgorged mucus she continued, "He's wondering if we found the body that fits the hand."

"Oh shit!" Nuru rolled off his bed and staggered over

to Gwendoline's personal computer, still feeling as if he might throw up but knowing he wouldn't. "What the shit? What the shit do you say to that?"

"Not sure. What do you think we should say?" She lay back in her bed; the sheets were still warm and she felt like taking another nap. How easy it would be for her to drop her whole life to start lying in bed full time.

"I don't know. I don't want to think about it really," said Nuru, also finding his way back into his bed.

"We'll think about it tomorrow."

* * *

Tomorrow came, and with it, no new messages on Gwendoline's personal computer. She wasn't sure how or when it happened, but she was almost back to her normal self. Nuru was feeling much better too. They ate breakfast. Today it was just scrambled eggs and some toast. They suspected anything stronger than that had the power to make things worse. After finishing their meal, Gwendoline felt as though she'd recaptured enough mental energy to resume their adventure. Nuru had also captured mental energy—mental energy to resume Gwendoline's adventure to which he was no longer attaching his name.

"Alright, so what do we say to Dwaine?" said Gwendoline as she put the breakfast dishes in the sink.

Nuru sat, still feeling a little hungry, and flicked a small bit of egg off the table in the general direction of the sink. "I don't know, ask him if *he* found out whose hand it was."

"Epic . . . so we take the snarky approach and be assholes." She grinned and hopped to her personal computer, pretending to say that in response.

"What about if we just be honest with him and say that

we figured out whose hand it was and that we returned it to its rightful owner? Also, I guess we didn't actually return it to its rightful owner, but saying that makes it seem more closed-case-like."

"That might be a better route. Seems like now would be a good time to entrap Dwaine into confessing about Darcy. We could tell him that we want him to confess to killing Darcy and then we tell him whose hand it is."

"That, uh, seems like," said Nuru, closing his eyes pretending to think with all his mental energy, "that seems like you're suggesting Dwaine will confess because of his own self-defeating curiosity? Sounds like we have a lotta leverage." He left deep thought mode and continued. "Plus, we still don't have any actual evidence that he actually did kill her."

Gwendoline started typing out her response. "I'm gonna say that we found out whose hand it was, but if he wants to know he's gonna have to tell us all he knows about how Darcy died. He obviously knows more than he let on. And also I'll say that we think he did it and lie and say that we have incriminating evidence against him."

"Sounds good." Nuru went over to the door and started putting on his shoes. He thought more clearly when wearing them.

"Christ, he's already responded." She stood up in excitement and put a foot up on the seat. "So I said 'Yeah, we know whose hand it is, but now we're trying to uncover the mystery of Darcy's death. We know you know about it, and we also think that you killed her based on evidence we've discovered. Let's meet up in person and get this sorted out.'" She paused to relish in a grin. "To which he said, 'I didn't kill Darcy you fuckers. Whose hand is it?

I'm trying to get on with my life here.'" She looked over at Nuru for a moment, her face grinning to the point that it almost hurt. Her personal computer beeped. "Oh shit, another message from him. 'I'm on my way to the city right now . . . let's meet up at the piss pot and I'll prove to you I didn't kill her . . . assholes.'"

"Sounds like Dwaine . . . oh God, what if the mayor actually killed Darcy? That'd be an embarrassing turn of events."

"Then at least you wouldn't feel obligated to give him back his hand."

Nuru returned to his chair with his shoes on. "Good point. Actually yeah, maybe I knew in my gut that he was the one who killed her and that's why I refused him hand access."

"You think we need to bring weapons with us? Like maybe a couple knives?"

"Well no, but I think it wouldn't hurt anything. Maybe an AR or a few grenades."

"I'm joking but also not joking I guess." She got up from her personal computer to put a jacket on. "I'm thinking I'll bring my Colt just to be safe." She walked over to the cupboard above the fridge and got down the pistol from behind an old box of graham crackers.

"Jesus you're actually bringing that? I mean I think I'm gonna bring a knife and that'll be the end of it. I don't wanna escalate things that much."

"This is last resort only."

They started for the only café Dwaine could've been referring to. Both hadn't left the livingspace in two days and the freshness of the air made them feel rejuvenated.

"He sounded pretty adamant that he wasn't the one

who killed Darcy. What if we have this totally wrong?" said Gwendoline.

"What if *you* have it way wrong. I wasn't the one who suggested that it was Dwaine. I think this is your narrative and your burden of proof."

"Yeah well maybe, but you certainly haven't objected too much until now."

Nuru did a dry spit take. "I think I've given you plenty a warning about how you could be wrong."

"Bullshit." Gwendoline glanced directly into the sun for a split second in anger. "Don't back out of this now, you're in it and if I'm wrong I'm dragging you down with me."

Silence now descended as they walked. The two passed Nuru's favorite sinkhole and it was hard for him to resist the urge to stop. After another twenty minutes of walking, they arrived at their destination. Dwaine's truck was parked outside and they could see him through the café window preparing a beverage. This particular café was exactly like the one they visited with the mayor except, for whatever reason, this one was always dirty on the outside and inside. Nuru had a theory that the person in charge of cleaning all the cafés didn't clean this one because they didn't like some regular patron and therefore left it gross and unkempt. Whatever the reason, the café was an anomaly of dirtiness within the community.

"This place matches Dwaine's aesthetic down to a T," said Gwendoline. "It's dirty on the outside, dirty on the inside, and no one ever visits it and when they do, something bad happens."

"Eh, I sorta got the vibe that he was a neat freak, but I know what you mean. Plus, I don't think I've had anything bad happen to me in this one, but today could be the first."

Dwaine looked up as they stepped into the building. He'd just finished putting the lid on his beverage and walked to a table. "I just wanna let you know right now that I forgive you for thinking I murdered Darcy. It's a completely understandable thought." Dwaine was wearing the exact same outfit he had on when they last saw him: two flannel shirts with the outer shirt's sleeves rolled up and oddly clean blue jeans. "I also wanna be completely transparent with you and say that I've been spying on you and know your exact movements of the last three days. But only your movements in public, technically. I have every right to do so for private purposes."

Nuru felt sick again but Gwendoline was unfazed. "If you were spying on us, well then how many fingers was I holding up yesterday at 10:22?"

"Probably none, you were probably asleep."

"Damn." Gwendoline went over to the ordering machine and got some herbal tea. She felt no tension between herself and Dwaine. Dwaine seemed relaxed, like he didn't have anything to hide. But maybe he was a sociopath. Nuru got an herbal tea too and sat down at Dwaine's table, one of the cleaner looking ones.

"So if you know what we've been up to, then you know we were at Darcy's house."

"Yes I do know that. I also know that you went in with a Geiger counter."

"So before we say anything, how about you now take the time to clear your name and prove to us that you didn't kill her," said Gwendoline. Even as she spoke, she was beginning to feel that maybe her theory wasn't as airtight as it was in her head.

Dwaine shifted in his chair, crossing his legs. "Eh, I

don't know. What's in it for me? I gotta know that you fuckwads aren't gonna try and fuck me over with what I say or something. You might bend my words and make some kind of gross-ass health bread."

"We won't do that . . . at least if you're not guilty," said Gwendoline.

Nuru was planning on speaking as little as possible on this trip. He sat and observed the dirty floor, counting the dead insects and trying to estimate how many years it had been since it was last cleaned.

"Well I don't think the issue is as black and white as you're making it out to be, to be honest with you." Dwaine hadn't touched his hot drink yet but now pulled out a flask from the front pocket of his inner flannel shirt. He smelled the flask's herbal aroma and took a sip. "You found out somehow that Darcy died of radiation poisoning, correct?"

"Yes."

"So then you also must have known that the most plausible location for the occurrence was at her home."

"Yes."

"How did you come to that conclusion is my question."

Gwendoline's face slanted. "How about you tell us what you know about it first and then we tell you."

"God you guys are fucking tough. I didn't frickin' kill her. Christ." He took another sip from the flask and placed it this time in his outer flannel shirt pocket. "All I know is that back before she got sick and died, I was working on a project involving some radioactive shit. Through several turns of events, things got mixed up and I lost track of a box I was using to store some materials. Never saw it again and had to get more of the stuff. A couple months later,

Darcy got sick and died. What I think happened was—and I only pieced this together after it was too late, mind you— that someone—who may or may not have been me—left the radioactive box sitting near someone else's shit at the Industrial Centre, only for a brief period of time. And someone—who may or may not have been me—was using a box that was not originally intended to house radioactive material and that may or may not have been mine. So then, someone who was named Darcy, takes the box with her to her house with some other shit for whatever reason and ends up exposing herself to radiation. The same radiation that you two seemed to get exposed to."

"What the fuck?" said Gwendoline. "Why the fuck would you do that? What? Like, what was running through your mind to lead you to do that?"

"Christ, I needed to clear some shit out of the way for like thirty seconds so I threw it in the box. How the fuck was I supposed to know that Darcy was gonna take it with her?"

"Well maybe because you were using a box that she owned?" said Gwendoline. She was getting worked up to the point where Nuru started to wonder if she'd pull out her pistol.

"Why the fuck didn't you say anything about it? Why didn't you say, 'Hey, there's radiation in there, don't go near it.'"

"I was in the fuckin' zone doing a bunch of crud!" He took a quick swig from the flask. "Yes, it is partially my fault that she died, but also, how was I supposed to know that she was gonna take the box?"

"Why didn't you tell her or alert anyone that the box was missing?"

"Well that's complicated." He put the flask back in his shirt pocket. "I wasn't technically supposed to be handling radioactive material at that time and it also may have been more than thirty seconds that I left the box sitting out and I may have not noticed it was gone until the next day and I may have wrongly assumed that the box had been moved by the hazmat bot."

"Goddammit that's so fucking negligent! What the hell is your problem?"

"I. Was. Busy. With. Shit! Something you two obviously know nothing about! And anyway, I can't take all the blame for this. Why the fuck did she take it with her? I don't know! She took some of my other shit too!"

"Goddamn." Gwendoline shook her head rapidly in short movements.

"But then after a day you never asked anyone where it was?"

"I asked everyone if they'd seen a box but no one—including Darcy—said they'd seen or moved it. So obviously I assumed the hazmat bot moved it into cold storage. It wasn't for another week that I resumed what I was doing with the radioactive material and went down there to find it missing. By that point it was too late anyway."

"God, you are such a piece of shit. Unbelievable."

"Oh give me a break, this kind of shit happens. She shouldn't have taken the box. Why would she take it anyway?"

"Maybe because she thought it was hers?" Gwendoline kept shaking her head. "So what you're telling me is that you didn't murder Darcy, but through your negligence she died."

"It was through a series of missteps from myriad

persons and technology that led to her death," said Dwaine, recovering from his own anger.

Gwendoline got up to get napkins anticipating a spilled beverage.

"I'm being honest with you right now. I had no intent of killing her and I had no thought that she was in danger after the box went missing. There's a bot that sweeps for radiation and contains objects and takes them to cold storage. I thought it picked it up and that was that. Yes, I was negligent, but the thought that she took the box never crossed my mind until I learned that she was sick. What was I supposed to say then? That she took my shit and got poisoned from it? Does anyone benefit from that?"

"Well she would've known what was causing her illness. She could've known that you were responsible for her death."

"Then she would've been angry at me, but that wouldn't have changed the fact that she was gonna die. Also, I am still only partially responsible for her death."

Gwendoline had been fidgeting with her calves and hit the table with her knees. Miraculously, no beverage spilled.

"What about her being able to get some closure? Maybe she would've forgiven you for what you did. Instead you let her suffer with mystery."

"Oh please, she knew what she had, she couldn't not have." He picked up his cup and set it back down. "She was exposed to radiation throughout her life. She thought it was finally catching up to her."

"Yeah, you bet, but you don't know. You fucking prick. Absolute prick."

"In hindsight, I think maybe I should've told her, but at the time I didn't think it would do anyone any good."

No one spoke for a minute or so. Nuru felt his body relax until Gwendoline spoke again, "The hand belonged to Anik, the mayor. He was in love with Darcy and cut it off to show how much he cared for her. She thought that it would save her life."

Dwaine restrained himself from speaking.

"You caused her immense pain and anxiety for the sole reason of you being a dipshit."

He took a drink from his flask—he had yet to take a sip of his hot beverage.

"Now where do we go from here?" said Gwendoline. "Where the fuck do we go from here?"

Dwaine polished off the flask and returned it to the pocket of his inner flannel shirt. "I think we just leave it. I think you take a step back to assess what's going on and then you realize that there's nothing you can do in this situation and then we move on."

Nuru's eyes moved from the grimy floor to Dwaine. Nuru did not understand this dude.

"What kind of redemption is there here? Yeah, I fucked up pretty badly which led to something terrible, but what can be done about it now?" Dwaine became remarkably sober. "There's just nothing to be done now. Everything that needs to be resolved is resolved. You can't do anything. I'm sorry."

He got up without his hot drink and walked out of the café. They heard a rumble as his truck came to life, then sounds of engine revs growing fainter and fainter.

"Goddammit." Gwendoline stood up. "That man has no soul."

"I'm thinking more and more that that's the case," said Nuru. He reached for Dwaine's hot beverage and smelled it. Hot water.

"Where do we go from here?" said Gwendoline. She nudged a sock wrapped around a chair at the adjacent table with her foot.

"Do you think we should tell the mayor?"

The sock had an interesting printed tessellation pattern that momentarily stole Gwendoline's attention. "I don't effing know. It seems like all we've done is stir the pot and haven't actually done anything good. I don't know what to do. It seems like telling the mayor would get him true closure, but also could potentially anger him a great deal and cause him even more emotional damage, and he's already been through enough."

"Sheeeuut . . ." said Nuru, moving his jaw horizontally back and forth in contemplation. There was silence again. He turned his attention to the sock Gwendoline had unwrapped from the chair leg. The more it was exposed the less pleasant it became.

"I think we're implicated in this now. I feel obligated to tell the mayor. I just don't know if that would be in his best interest . . . I feel bad." She went to the ordering machine and stared at it.

"We've stirred the pot, that's for sure."

"Goddammit, Dwaine. I don't even know how I would've reacted if he said he *did* kill Darcy."

"Can we leave?"

"Yeah, let's get outta here."

CHAPTER TWENTY-FIVE

They departed the café and Nuru steered them to Sink-hole Twelve so he could think things through on his own grimy turf. He took a seat in his washing machine throne. "So just to recap, we've figured out whose hand it was, got severe radiation sickness, and then found out that a person we recently met accidentally killed someone."

"Yeah, that's about right," said Gwendoline as she scrambled to where she remembered finding the broken fish tank.

"And now we're left with the dilemma of whether we should tell the mayor about it."

"Yeah."

"So what do you think?"

"I don't know." She found the broken fish tank; it looked different than she remembered.

"Same pretty much." The thought of the mayor in this setting caused Nuru to remember their invitation to the next community event. "Oh, what are we gonna do about the community event that he invited us to? The lawn bowling thing but with beach balls. God, that'd be a cruddy place to learn that your lover was killed by some horsehole coworker."

"I don't know. At first I was thinking that we have an obligation to tell him, but now I don't know if we do."

"What about that guy we talked to after we were done scoping out that house? I feel like there's an eighty-five percent chance that he's gonna talk to someone and that the mayor is going to find out that we were there. I mean let's be honest, the mayor probably already knows. Why wouldn't he? All the goddamn people in this place know each other and they all talk about this kinda shit. It's good conversation. What else is there to talk about?"

"You think that?" said Gwendoline. "I think he doesn't know and never will unless we tell him."

"Yeah." Nuru frowned. "What I'm thinking is that he's gonna find out we've been snooping and we've already made that bad decision. What's left now is for him to either find out via us, or by second or third hand."

"In your defense, you're probably correct." She reached down and touched the glob of homogenized plastic rocks from the fish tank but didn't register their sensation. "We may have gone in far enough to where it's only a matter of time that he'll find out. God, I hate it when you're right. The thing to do is just tell him. Or what we could do, is tell him a modified version of the story." She grinned nervously, knowing she didn't have the guts to do that.

"Yeah that'd be a really smart idea. Let's say that we went in to see if we could find the source of the radiation and then say that we didn't? Or, we could say that we found it and there was a letter written by her that said she put it there herself. Both of those stories would work."

"So we tell him that it was Dwaine? I feel like that could have really bad consequences if stated inaccurately or incorrectly."

"We tell him there was a box mix-up at the Industrial Centre and she brought the wrong box of stuff back with her."

"That could work. It would be leaving out certain information though. I think he'd have questions as to how the boxes became mixed up. We could tell him we didn't know."

"So, we're essentially just bringing up a painful memory

that he's tried to forget and answering some questions but then posing more. So we're essentially just stressing the mayor out because we wanted to figure out whose hand it was." Nuru flicked the side of a washing machine with the intention of making his finger hurt.

"The thing is, yes, we're stirring up the bottom of the river, but we were not the ones who did all this shit. We're the messengers—people don't shoot those people."

"Except the messengers were active in stirring up the trouble and weren't sent by some higher power."

She leaned against an old car hood near the fish tank. "We were sent by Dwaine. He could've told some bogus story about the hand if he wanted to."

"I don't know if that logic is completely in alignment with actual logic."

"So," Gwendoline slid off the hood and carefully walked to where Nuru was sitting, "we tell him all that we know and what happens? He's finally at peace."

"Yes, or he tries to fucking kill Dwaine or something. What the frick is stopping that from happening?"

"Uh, probably nothing actually. I think that scenario is very likely to occur if we did a poor job telling the mayor about how it went down."

"And too, we could say that Dwaine knew what caused her to die but since he didn't know the mayor, he kept the information to himself since there was no need to share."

"That could work."

Nuru got up and sighed. He started walking out of the sinkhole instinctively heading to their livingspace. Gwendoline watched him walk all the way out before departing. As Gwendoline ascended, she smelled the air get fresher and fresher and drier and drier. She saw that Nuru had stopped and was looking at something, waiting for her to get up to pace with him.

"Actually, you know we should just head to the mayor's house right now, and get it out of the way." She sighed and looked at where Nuru was looking. He must have been staring at nothing.

"Alright. Well, if you think it's best, then we'll do it." They doubled back briefly, setting path for the mayor's house. As they walked, both felt painfully aware of their oversights. Before starting the whole investigation, Gwendoline, for whatever reason, thought she'd never be in a position where the consequences of her actions would weigh on her conscience. Every step she'd thought ahead, but she never considered the most probable outcome, in hindsight. Her death was just a workplace accident.

This differed from Nuru's sullen thoughts. While he did become engulfed in blind-adventure ecstasy at points, he'd always remained skeptical of their decision-making, but had offered no alternative. Dwaine was right: there would be nothing good to come of telling anyone.

Gwendoline didn't believe keeping silent would help. Telling the mayor would be the right thing to do; an apology was in order.

They arrived at the mayor's house but only a non-human came to the door when they knocked. "Louis!" said Nuru. "Louis! Is Anik home, Louis?" They heard claws hit the wooden floor from the dog stamping his paws in excitement. He didn't bark.

"I guess we'll have to go to City Hall and start a scene there," said Gwendoline. She peeked inside the window to the left of the door. Louis noticed right away and scampered over, his tail wagging quickly as he panted, head bobbing up and down from the force of each breath. "What a good dog!" They started walking to City Hall.

"I'm starting to think this whole thing was a mistake." He looked up at the sky and then at Gwendoline and then at a blue house. The house had a four-wheeler out front.

"I'm starting to think you thought that from the beginning."

"Good point, so I guess I'm in the clear then."

"I wouldn't go that far." She laughed.

City Hall was located near the center of the community, an area with a handful of other non-residential buildings. The community had no collective name for this zone and everyone referred to it as something different. For example, the mayor called it the City Centre, but Gwendoline and Nuru called it downtown. They took the road which traveled through this section of the community. It was one of the busiest roads with vehicles passing them every few minutes. They passed a friend of Nuru's transporting an excavator. It was almost noon and the sun made most surfaces bright except when it would occasionally disappear behind a cloud. The houses glimmered ever so slightly when they were touched by the light. The air was its familiar dryness.

Gwendoline wanted to get her mind off the upcoming conversation. She hadn't thought about anything else but "the case" in what seemed like forever. She'd broken a personal rule by stepping away from an art project while it was still in development mode. She struggled to remember which themes she wanted to capture in the painting and started to doubt as to whether she'd actually thought of any. The painting was to be her standing in front of the diamonds. The ground was to be composed of various textures compiled from what she'd seen within the community. The sky was going to be simple, for now. What a time consuming affair this was.

"I'm thinking about that painting again." Nuru was busy staring at the mountains and didn't respond. "I'm trying to visualize how to paint diamonds since they're mostly made up of refractive elements. I would have to paint—or, have the opportunity to paint—the weird ground textures within the diamond all distorted and weird looking. That is, if I would want to paint the diamonds in a realistic way. I don't know if I want to do that though. The painting will have elements of surrealism maybe, I haven't decided. What I could do is introduce a theme where, within the diamond, we see people and objects that don't exist in either the sky or the ground. They would be more or less illusions or just ghosts trapped within the diamond. That would add an element of depth, something like representing the unseen as opposed to only representing the seen-but-not-acknowledged."

"Seems like you could do something like that. Could put Dwaine all distorted with chromatic aberrations around him—no big deal with that lingo by the way—trapped in one. Maybe, I don't know."

She exhaled and looked down the street they were passing. "I don't know either. What would exist between what is seen and what is not seen here? Something people only catch glimpses of a moment at a time, something that relates to who *we* are? Abstractions or thoughts? Might be something I gotta think about longer."

"Yeah probably. I couldn't tell you that. I think," he paused, "don't people do that kinda shit with history? Like our ancestors are in the clouds or built into the streets?"

"Yeah, I don't know if that's what I'm thinking it would be, but also I don't know what I'm going for."

They were nearing City Hall. Without her consent, Gwendoline's mind shifted again to meeting with the mayor. Nuru hoped Gwendoline would do most of the talking and take most of the blame. He was the better talker and would refrain from getting as intense as Gwendoline would, but Gwendoline, even if she was more forceful, could be more articulate with her words, giving the mayor a more accurate explanation of what happened.

City Hall was blue and bigger than its residential counterparts of the same color. Near it, a sign attached to two poles stuck into the ground reading, "Community City Hall." Near the sign was a flagpole with no flag. The building had two windows on either side of its double doors and had a slanted roof designed for snow to slide off to the back of the building. They went in and followed a sign directing them to the left, meeting a person who told them Anik was probably eating lunch and could likely be found out back. They circled to the building's reverse and saw him sitting on the curb with his feet in the parking lot. Prior to seeing the two approach, he'd been staring at his shoes. He looked at the two approaching and stared past them. A jar of peanut butter with a silver utensil sticking out of it sat next to him. Over his shoulder was a broken window. The mayor's non-prosthetic hand was covered in blood.

CHAPTER TWENTY-SIX

Dwaine's thoughts cleared as he drove back to the Industrial Centre after his meeting with the two justice crusaders. He was no longer angry and something inside him started to rise in his brain. He'd planned to return to the Industrial Centre and continue his activities, confident that the two would drop the issue, but as he drove, the thought that he could be mistaken grew and grew. It was in his best interest to tell the mayor himself about how Darcy died before they could. He couldn't tell if this idea was rooted in damage control or righting his conscience. He hated leaving things halfway, but Gwendoline calling him a prick and an asshole was starting to bug him. He made it just under a mile before he yanked the wheel and turned the truck around for City Hall. He momentarily considered that, while being the right choice morally, it may be wrong to do this as he felt the alcohol hit his system. He knew he could still drive fine though; drinking made him more relaxed, and honest.

He arrived at City Hall, parking his truck in the back lot. He used to be a regular and knew the route to bypass the secretary. He found Anik at his desk working on something resembling a sketch of two people standing under a tree.

"Hey, Anik!" The mayor looked up and saw Dwaine's face unconvincingly smiling at him. The mayor didn't know how to react. The mayor looked at him and nodded. He put down his pen. "I suppose you probably know why I'm here," Dwaine continued.

"Something related to my hand I suppose." Contrary to Nuru's suspicions, the prying neighbor never brought up the "fungus testing people" as a conversation starter, so the mayor was not aware of any of the two's activities.

"Yes, tangentially I suppose." Dwaine looked on edge, still standing in the doorway.

The mayor wearily picked up on Dwaine's body language, "Why don't we go outside and talk. I'll take an early lunch." Anik felt as if he was going to need fresh air for this conversation. Maybe not fresh air as much as natural light, something he lacked in his office that aided to his constant feeling of claustrophobia.

"Sure, works for me!"

The mayor opened the top drawer of a filing cabinet behind his desk and pulled out a spoon. He grabbed the jar of peanut butter sitting on top of the cabinet and followed Dwaine out back. They stood outside leaning against the building. It was a beautiful day. Anik opened the peanut butter and put a spoonful into his mouth, assuming Dwaine would begin talking immediately.

"You heard that two people came out to the Industrial Centre and I gave 'em a tour." Anik nodded. "I gave them a tour of the facility which included an area which may or may not be known by the public, an area I didn't know you knew about."

Anik nodded again, his mouth still housing remnants of the first spoonful of peanut butter.

"Before I proceed, I want to stress again that I didn't know who you were before this happened." Dwaine paused and looked at the mayor with his lips loosely together, like a frown using no muscles. The mayor nodded. "From them just earlier today I learned that you were seeing Darcy. They got it into their heads that I killed her, which I did not do." Anik rubbed the roof of his mouth with his tongue trying to get the rest of the peanut butter down his throat. Dwaine was unnerved by the mayor's expression, forgetting that he'd just put in a large spoon of peanut butter. "I understand as well that you were aware to some extent what caused her illness, that she got radiation poisoning from somewhere." Dwaine looked at the mayor. He stared blankly at Dwaine. Anik's body was anticipating going into shock. He felt a tingling in his hand and arms, like his blood was being replaced by a gas lighter than air, helium maybe. "I would've told you this had I known that you were such a big part of Darcy's life, but somehow I wasn't aware of that." Dwaine wasn't sure if that was true, but it was in the majority of scenarios he'd run through in his head, maybe.

"She got the dose from a radioactive crate that got accidentally taken from the Industrial Centre and placed in her attic. I was aware the crate had gone missing, but due to a faulty train of thought on my end, I never considered that it would've gone to her home. I didn't know where the crate had ended up until those two said they'd found radiation after going into Darcy's house. And yes, when she started to get sick, I realized that she must have taken the box, but by that point it was too late." He paused, not knowing where he should go from here. He'd started to feel a sense of genuine guilt as he spoke. It looked like Anik didn't know how to feel. Dwaine could see in the mayor's eyes that he was going to speak and Dwaine decided to talk before the mayor could ask any pressing questions. "And I'm going to be one hundred percent clean with you, the event was set in motion by something I was experimenting on, which I should have handled in a more secure way."

Anik didn't say anything. Dwaine had admitted some guilt, but was obviously being careful in picking his words. "I suppose that kind of stuff can happen out there," Anik finally said.

"Yes, unfortunately that's part of the job." Dwaine

flinched. Oops, bad answer, his tone came across too much like an off-the-hook sigh of relief. He'd fallen into Anik's trap.

Anik exhaled deeply through his nose and squatted down to set the jar of peanut butter on the ground. He got up, walked to the back door of City Hall and calmly punched his hand through the door's window. He started bleeding immediately. Dwaine looked at him not knowing what to say while Anik didn't know what to think. Anik's flash of adrenaline was now over and he started to feel the warm liquid drip off his hand. He sat down on the curb and folded his arms. Blood started trickling down his elbows and onto the side of his pants. Dwaine stepped into the parking lot to face the mayor.

"I'm sorry, I don't know how you feel and will never know how you feel. I'm sorry that you weren't aware sooner and I'm especially sorry that—due to me along with other factors—that someone you loved died." Dwaine felt a sensation he hadn't felt in a long time. It was a feeling that made him feel like he was somehow connected to Anik, experiencing his pain. It made him feel sad—sadness and guilt. He felt numb too, but that was probably due to the alcohol he'd consumed. "Hopefully you can forgive me, and know that this misstep has only happened once." Anik looked up at him but didn't say anything. It was safe to assume that the phrase "only happened once" was too much. "You need me to take you to the Heath Centre?" Anik shook his head and looked down at the ground. After seeing the blood that had started to pool on the ground, Anik suddenly felt a deep hunger, as if his stomach awoke from hibernation, and he reached for the jar of peanut butter. His hand started bleeding more intensely as he dug the spoon into the jar. Dwaine didn't know what to say and watched the mayor eat two spoonfuls before he spoke.

"I'm glad you've told me this. I will need time to process this information. I have many emotions and would like to be alone to process them."

"Sure," said Dwaine. "I'll be at the Industrial Centre if you need to contact me. Whatever you want, just let me know. I understand if you want me dead or whatever. Just let me know."

He went over to his truck, now regretting taking up three parking spaces, and drove out of the lot. "Well that went about as good as it could've gone," Dwaine said to himself and sighed. He relaxed as he drove and let the alcohol wash over him. He ran his bumper into a table saw while pulling into the Industrial Centre and it let him know it was time to kill the engine. He'd take the rest of the day to relax.

CHAPTER TWENTY-SEVEN

The mayor sat in a pool of his own blood. It seemed like he'd been sitting there only a minute before the two young people showed up, even if it had been closer to a half hour. He wondered what they were planning on saying. He wasn't sure if he wanted to hear it or not. He didn't know how he felt. His body hurt, but he felt like a yoke had been lifted from his shoulders only for a new, different one to be put in its place. This weight felt less heavy but more cold, like his skin was hardening from the frozen yoke. He couldn't gauge how responsible Dwaine was for Darcy's death, but he believed it was an accident. Maybe it didn't matter what degree of responsibility Dwaine carried.

"What happened?" said Gwendoline, eyeing the mayor's hand. She walked the difference between him at a pace barely below a jog with Nuru following suit. Anik looked at them and then looked straight ahead. After a moment, he twitched his head away and then brought it to them.

"I punched the wrong hand through the glass."

"You need us to get you to the Heath Centre?" asked Nuru even though he knew the answer was going to be no. Anik had lost a lot of blood, but his injury was the type that would heal if he allowed it to. It didn't seem he wanted it to, or rather, he was still hungry and continued to eat from the jar of peanut butter every couple minutes, reopening his lacerations.

"No, I don't think so."

"You sure?" asked Gwendoline. She took a step forward to him and backed up, unsure what to do. "I think it might be smart if you went to get that looked at."

Anik realized the two weren't going to leave him alone so he alerted them to the location of a first aid kit. Nuru ran inside to get it.

After a moment of silence with Gwendoline's concerned face staring at him, he took another scoop from the jar causing his nearly clotted wounds to open again as he clenched the spoon. "Dwaine stopped by." He put the peanut butter into his mouth and let his tongue work. Gwendoline remained silent. "He told me what you guys were up to." His mouth was still full of peanut butter and his words came out mushy. Gwendoline said nothing. Anik got the majority of the peanut butter down his throat and continued. "He told me you guys thought he killed Darcy and he apologized for his part leading to her death." He paused to clear out the whole of his mouth. "That you two broke into her house and found the source of the radiation."

"Yeah."

"I don't know how I feel. On one hand, I feel like killing Dwaine. On the other, I feel like letting it go to realize that spending time in the Industrial Centre is—and was—intrinsically dangerous. And that of all the people who worked there, everyone else except for him is dead. At least I think that's the case . . . I don't know what to think." It was strange to see a man who'd hit rock bottom many times in his life still look unaccustomed to the feeling. Blood followed the same path down his arm, re-wetting the streaks only allowed to partially cake. They heard the sound of metal hit wood as Nuru kicked the door and appeared with the first aid kit already opened. He tossed it on the ground letting its contents spill having already found the wrap.

"Alright. Open up your hand," said Nuru. "Don't do it fast."

Nuru wrapped the mayor's hand tight and sat facing him. He looked at Nuru and then at his hand with an expressionless face.

"There must be some force wanting me to not have the use of my hands, and maybe I'm in cahoots with it." His tone read as an earnest muse of the idea, perhaps truly believing it.

"Listen, I'm sorry we dug into Darcy," said Gwendoline. "You can think whatever you want of us. From what we saw, we—I—felt like it needed to be solved. I'm sorry we opened this again after you'd moved on. Now I see—and Nuru and I talked about this earlier—that we maybe got pulled in without seeing the bigger picture."

"Don't worry about it," said Anik. "I don't really blame you. I can't sit here and not think a part of me wanted to do that, to solve it. Maybe I could've if I'd thought about it more. How fucking daft I was to not even consider the house."

Gwendoline was new to the act of consoling but knew she had to speak. Her voice didn't sound convincing. "Don't beat yourself up over it. It's not your fault."

"There are mental workings in me that I don't understand. I think knowing or not knowing certain information will help me be happy but that's never the case. I worry now—now that I begin the process of forgiveness with Dwaine, and once the last detail about her death is known to me—that I won't be any happier than I am now or ever was for that matter. I don't know what I'm saying. It's almost like I have no control over how I feel. Events wash over me and I interpret them in different ways depending on my mood, rather than events affecting it. I can't see a way forward but I know the way forward." Anik grunted, starting to stand up but felt light-headed and slammed back down to the curb.

"You want me to bring out a chair?" asked Nuru.

"No, no."

"Ok, sure."

"I don't remember why I was gonna stand in the first place." He let a breath escape his nose. "I don't know how I feel. It's like some things are distractions and some things are not distractions and I can't parse which are which. The line is blurry, as all lines are when your vision is poor."

Gwendoline looked at him, thinking it was her turn to talk but wasn't sure how to proceed. She worried the mayor could still be a danger to himself but didn't know what the two of them could do. Instead, she considered what he said. "I guess you could see the past week and a half as a distraction from our lives." She realized her remark could sound as if she was leveling her own emotions to his in a way that could be interpreted as confrontational and continued, "I mean in that it distracted me from working on the crap that I work on. But the thing is, the painting was just a distraction to keep my mind sane. I'm . . . I'm not saying that I've experienced what you have, I'm just following up on the idea you proposed."

"That's fine. I understand what you mean. The painting is an object that allows you to keep your mind occupied so your mind does not devour itself. That's why anyone does anything. It's food into the stomach. We don't think about sadness when we have other things to worry about. I get that. It takes the mind off of our anxieties, a modern problem. We have too many resources available to us so we no longer have to survive. It frees our brains that were not created for idling in such a way. Maybe in a thousand years that'll change."

"That's what I was getting at, yeah. But when there's no mystery nor painting, what is there then? When there's no distraction."

Anik breathed out his nose. He was starting to realize that his hand was in immense pain. "I know you say that rhetorically, since that's the question that everyone reaches at some point, and I clearly don't have an answer. The best answer I can give you is that it is *to live*. Living *is* the distraction, like that old quote or whatever. You have to assign meaning to the object. I guess for me I refuse to assign that meaning to the basis of my existence."

Gwendoline didn't know what to say. She'd never had

thoughts like this in any serious capacity outside of blasé academic discussions. Neither suffered like the mayor did.

"Maybe that sounds too harsh, although I think it's true," said Anik. "The meaning of life is just to live or something. But that's not good enough for me I guess. What would that make this peanut butter or Darcy? Just objects within life? I don't know, maybe meanings compound. Maybe these topics have been addressed in self-help books but I can't bother to read those." He looked at Nuru. "Maybe the distractions are the meaning and whether they're good or bad, it doesn't matter." Nuru wasn't sure if he was supposed to respond to that, but Anik thankfully wasn't done. "Life can be filled with meaning, but possibly contain no happiness. And that's sad, supposedly. Maybe me punching the window was some sort of innate reaction within me, a survival mechanism, telling me, 'You will be consumed by your thoughts if you do not find a distraction now!' That worked. I have a non-life-threatening injury and can think about that rather than what fucking Dwaine said. I'm talking a lot. Maybe I'm getting punchy, no pun intended. God, if this is my idea of punchy, I wonder what I'm like when I'm not punchy." Anik tried to get up, this time helped by Nuru. He stumbled over to a bucket flipped upside down against the metal siding of City Hall and sat. "I think I'm gonna take the rest of the day off. I'm not sure if I'm up for walking back to my place though. Not sure how I'm gonna get back."

"Are you okay?" asked Gwendoline. She felt embarrassed asking but quickly got over it. "Like, actually okay? You're not gonna try and hurt yourself?"

"I'll be fine."

"We'll get you a ride home and how about this, we'll stay with you for awhile and make sure you're feeling better and that your hand is okay. Take Louis out a bit."

"I'd appreciate the ride but I don't know if you're needed at my home." Something in him refused to admit that he'd like it if they stayed.

Walking inside City Hall, Nuru turned and said he'd get one of his parents to pick them up. He returned a moment later and said a ride will be there in three minutes.

"You think you could get me some water?" he said to Nuru. Anik handed him his bloody jar of peanut butter, still about a third full. "Fill this up with water from the sink in the lounge." Nuru couldn't help flashing his eyes at Gwendoline to see her reaction to Anik's request. She was expressionless. He quickly returned and handed the jar back to Anik. "Thanks," he said, taking a sip of the water with his good hand. "I don't want you to feel guilty about what you've done. I don't think there's a reason. You seem like you've learned from the experience and won't repeat the same mistakes again. Maybe not though, sometimes treading lightly can be something one regrets when it comes to dealing with people. Sometimes people need a jolt." He finished the water. For as hastily as Nuru had wrapped his hand, the wound had not reopened, even when Anik used it to set the jar back down. Nuru smiled at his handiwork but immediately felt guilty about it. No one spoke until Nuru's mom pulled up in a work vehicle.

Over the phone, Nuru had told her what had happened and stressed to his mother not to ask if Anik needed to go to the Health Centre. She kept her promise as they loaded him in. When they arrived at Anik's house, Nuru's mom privately forced Nuru to affirm that they'd keep an eye on the mayor. She left after receiving the affirmation and the two helped Anik to the door.

"You think you can grab my keys out of my side jean pocket?" asked Anik.

"Yeah, I can." Nuru fished out the mayor's keys from his pocket dried through and stuck together with blood. They could hear Louis panting heavily on the other side of the door.

"Make sure that dog doesn't knock me over. You think you can oversee him do his business outside?"

"Yes to both," said Nuru. He got the door unlocked and held onto Anik's arm as Louis rushed out, his tail wagging greeting his friends. It was exciting to see them again, and at such an unexpected time! However, Louis noticed something alien on his slow moving companion's hand, but had higher priorities outdoors at the moment. Gwendoline lead Anik into the house and sat him down in his chair.

"I think I'm gonna be alright. I think I might rest a little bit. You can stay here if you want to but don't feel obligated."

"I think we'll stay for awhile just to make sure you don't die of blood loss."

"Nah, I'll be fine. Although I'm not sure I'll be able to fall asleep." He closed his eyes and reclined the chair. As he did, Louis burst through the door, running into his companion's elevated feet. Anik opened his eyes and un-reclined the chair to scratch Louis's head. "Hi, Louis! You're probably wondering why I'm back so early today!" Louis, in fact, was wondering that. His companion appeared to be in pain and that made Louis feel sad. Louis realized that this was a different type of pain though, more uncommon than previous pains, pain his companion would recover from. Louis was curious as to what the thing on his companion's hand tasted like and gave it a lick. He didn't like the taste. Anik smiled. "I bet that tastes pretty bad." He dismissed the dog with his leg and closed his eyes again to see if he could fall asleep. Curiously enough, he was able to quite quickly. When he started snoring, Nuru motioned to Gwendoline that he was going outside to get some air.

The two sat on the front step, propping the door so it wouldn't lock them out. Louis ambled over, sticking his nose through the cracked door and Gwendoline let him out. They watched Louis mill about smelling various things of interest and tasting bits of dirt. Louis was always happy outside and very glad his companion came back early. He was a pure and joyous dog. "So what do you think we should do?" said Nuru as he watched the dog eat some vegetation.

"I think we wait until Louis wants to go back in and then check on the mayor and then dip out." As if on cue, Louis stopped his sniffing and lay down on the ground. He looked at them with his tongue out, panting slowly. His dark eyes content, still without clouds of age. "I'm worried I'm gonna be haunted by Anik's view of the world, that everything is a distraction." She duck-walked over from the step to Louis and started petting him. Louis found it quite pleasing. "I guess me thinking about it is a distraction."

"It may not be the healthiest way to think," said Nuru, staying where he was.

"There are just a lot of ways to view the world and none of them are satisfying."

"Too open-ended."

"Maybe—God I'm sorry to go back to this but I can't help myself—the idea of philosophy and scientific advancement are just other ways to distract us from not going crazy."

"I think you're starting to extrapolate the words of a guy who just punched his hand through a window."

"Yeah I know, but it's still interesting." Louis rolled onto his back to get some belly scratch action. As she scratched, his tail oscillated speeding up and slowing down at the same rate of Gwendoline's scratching. "I think I'm gonna have to put Mr. Louis into my painting!" Mr. Louis thought that was a grand idea, whatever she said. The three stayed outside for another ten minutes before Nuru got impatient and checked on Anik, declaring it safe for them to leave. Louis was sad to go indoors, but happy when he remembered his companion was home.

"I may be wrong, but I think the mayor needs a vacation," said Nuru as he closed the door.

"I don't know what he needs."

"Let's go past the floaty things even if it's not really on the way back."

"Sounds like a plan."

They followed a route that took them past the floaty things but they didn't stop. Nuru merely wanted more time to let thoughts unfold in his mind. They arrived at the livingspace by midafternoon.

"My God how can it only be fourteen fucking hours right now?" said Gwendoline looking at the clock. "Oh wow, I totally spaced that I had my pistol with me this whole time too." She laughed and took it out from her jacket. "Glad I didn't have to use it." She tossed it back in the cupboard. "Oh, speaking of forgetting things, did anyone tell anyone at City Hall that Anik was gonna be gone this afternoon?"

"Eh, not really. I told the secretary person that he'd hurt himself but not that he wasn't gonna be back. I'll send a message to the desk there." He sat at his personal computer and composed a message, excluding that the wall was intentionally punched. "Sent."

"I guess I'm gonna start doing some sketches. Seems like this whole incident is wrapped up."

"Ah yes," said Nuru, swiveling away from his screen. "The familiar feeling of emptiness sets in. We've finished the television season, or, the Archive section on cute extinct mammals. The void is back and needs filling." He was serious, this being something he regularly experienced after finishing a topic on the Archive, but was mostly trying to provoke Gwendoline back into the idea of distractions—*distraction theory.*

"We do get sorta a high from stuff like that. It's not false. How easy it is to get sidetracked . . ." Something snapped in her mind and she found herself burned out talking about that crap. She entered her drawing area and looked at what she had sketched out for the next painting. Not very much. "This is almost a chore to come back to right now."

"No need to start this second. Take some time to relax, take it all in. You don't have a deadline or anything."

"Oh fuck off with your 'you don't have a deadline' garbage," she said, turning away from her drawing area and sitting down on the couch. "The deadline is life and I need to produce something before I die."

"Do you?"

She tilted her head back and let it roll around on her shoulders. "I don't know. Seems like a waste though."

"It's only a waste if you think it's a waste," said Nuru with a hint of condescension.

She flicked her eyes at him without moving her head and then directed her gaze out the window. "Fuck off with that shit."

BOOK II

Five months later, it was winter. The sky was black; light only came from the bulbs attached to buildings illuminating the ground. Gwendoline finished her painting in the fall and Nuru continued reading whatever he felt like, today it was about aardvarks. Their lives between summer and winter consisted of activities only of interest to them. They still went for walks, but as it got colder, their lengths shortened. Neither heard from Dwaine nor Anik apart from a short interaction with the latter at the community beach ball lawn-bowling event where they had vowed to appear. Anik seemed to be about the same as he'd been when they first met him. He'd thanked the two for helping him find *true* closure, something he said he realized he didn't have before.

When they walked, their feet interacted with the frozen ground and made familiar winter noises, crunching and squeaking, the sound of a sweeping broom as their boots swung through delicate water crystallizations. The feeling of warm toes that still feel cold and calloused from being frozen was nearly always present in them.

Now, they sat in the livingspace doing nothing interesting. Nuru was reading and Gwendoline was thinking about something that had been bugging her since she finished her latest painting. What is the least technical art medium? It certainly couldn't be painting. The signal to noise ratio—from thought/emotion to art object/ emotional reaction—of all artistic mediums that she'd considered were all rather technical. Perhaps the technical ease of the medium depends on the feeling one is trying to convey. These were the thoughts of a person in their quarter-life crisis with nothing better to do. Gwendoline's personal computer made a noise and she glanced over at it from the couch. "Cripes, it's Dwaine!"

"How come he always messages you and not me?"

She threw her blanket aside as she got up to read the message. "Oh wow." She put her lips together and half frowned.

"What's it say?"

"Attention Gwendoline and also Nuru, I have developed a major sickness the likes of which I will not recover from. I ask of the two of you a favor. Later today I will be killing myself in such a way as to not inconvenience you—since I know you're both very busy—with having to dispose of my body. But, I've decided to include you in my 'will,' which is moderately clandestine since the Industrial Centre technically isn't mine, but that's beside the point. The point is, I've left a map of the black sites and navigational instructions on the dashboard of my truck. I know that we don't know each other well and that you probably both hate me, but you seem like good enough people and I'd hate for the Centre's many wonders to be lost to time. More importantly, there's a small chance that my death could tangentially trigger a fire. If you would be so kind as to come out and make sure that such an event doesn't happen, that would be great since the fire prevention system has been disabled. Cheers, Dwaine. P.S. I checked all other areas of the Centre and found no other hands." Gwendoline squinted at the text and bit part of her lower lip. "Not to be rude to the soon-to-be-dead, but what an asshole. Does he really need to make us come out there?"

"Give him a break," said Nuru, stretching his arms from his bed. "He's right in that we don't have that much going on. Plus, it's not like he knew anyone. That being said, I do agree with you that he's made things more difficult than needed. Also he's got some superiority thing going on. Didn't he say how much he wanted the place to be a tourist attraction? But at the same time, he hid from the public God knows how many rooms full of cool shit like pirate's treasure or whatever. I guess we'll have to find out."

"Yeah, if that's the case and there are other rooms like the cistern, maybe we could open it up. Although that may not be possible if there's a giant fusion reactor sitting on top of everything."

"I think that seems like the right thing to do in this situation."

She stood up from the screen. "I guess should we be off? You think it's safe to walk there?"

Nuru was rather comfortable in his bed at the moment and exhaled deeply. "I'd rather not, what's the temp out there anyway?"

She looked out the window at the thermometer taped to a piece of wood they'd jammed into the ground. "Says it's like negative twelve right now. No wind though."

"What time is it?"

"14:53."

"And it's gonna take us like an hour to get there on foot. Ugh. That bastard better've filled up the tank on that truck 'cuz I don't wanna walk back."

"There's no way that'll start once we get it back here. Then we'll have some oversized truck sitting outside of the place until it warms up. He's gotta have some other vehicles out there. There's no way they don't have a fleet of snow machines or an actually usable modern transport vehicle."

"What a dickbag for this," he said as he pushed himself out of bed, starting for his boots.

"I'm gonna make sure to bring my PC_X with me in case we get stranded."

"I'll bring mine too. God, my dad would crap his pants at the opportunity to pick us up two miles outside city limits. Hopefully that won't happen."

"Hopefully that *does* happen now that you say it." Gwendoline grinned as she slid a balaclava over her head, causing her hair to become saturated with static electricity.

"We'll call the mayor before we call my dad."

The two entered the outdoors. It was still. They saw no movement. Nuru spoke loudly in order to penetrate the insulation surrounding Gwendoline's ears, "Well here we go, slowly entering the blackness."

Gwendoline looked straight ahead, also speaking loudly, "Against our will."

"Eh, not really. We could've backed out at any time. We had a choice."

"Yeah I suppose so. 'Twas us who picked this path."

"Back out of autopilot maybe."

"Yeah maybe."

Since having to yell to hear one another, conversation from that point was kept to a minimum. Surrounded by darkness as they exited the city limits, Nuru was still somewhat frightened by the level of black, even after experiencing it for his whole life. "This is the closest thing to a hellscape I've ever seen."

"What?"

"It's a hellscape out here," he said, louder.

"Yeah."

They took the same route they did last time, paralleling the private access road. A faint glow in the distance let them know how far away they were from the Centre. No landmarks around them were visible; the darkness was near impenetrable.

Stepping into the decidedly not-on-fire building was welcome. The first portion of the building looked exactly how they remembered and they quickly moved through it to survey Dwaine's work area. It looked nothing like it had. It was now an open space resembling the room's original intent, a hangar, more than a cluttered workshop full of tools and industrial objects. All tools had vanished with the exception of three that were lined up against the east wall. The former centerpiece of the workshop, the cubes of concrete, were no longer present. Gwendoline snorted when she saw the wood-fired pizza oven and ingredient station still set up. "Of fucking course he left the pizza shit up."

Nuru instinctively shook his head with a smile somewhere between disbelief and irony. "I mean, why wouldn't he? Heck, he probably used the oven to burn his body."

"Nah, I'm guessing he locked himself in a crypt he made from those cement blocks."

"Oh yeah, that makes more sense actually. I wonder how he did it." Nuru stepped down the stairs from the platform overlooking the former workshop to scope out the pizza station.

"I wonder what made him get sick." Gwendoline followed him down the stairs but went to Dwaine's pickup parked diagonally in the middle of the hangar. Nuru caught up with her after affirming that a pizza—or two—could still be made.

"Probably some sort of radiation-related thing is my guess," said Nuru, "For all we know, he could've gone out to Darcy's house and stolen back that old nuclear fuel to finish his experiment or whatever."

"That would be amazing and actually very believable," she paused, "fitting even. But maybe it had something to do with him always wearing two shirts."

The truck was unlocked, or rather, didn't have locks. She climbed in and took the stack of papers along with a small encrypted storage device sitting on top. Taped to the device was a piece of paper that read 'woodfiredpizzaislife.' She connected it to her PC_X and entered the password. "Nice. Got all the maps now. She handed the storage device to Nuru and started unfolding the papers, letting them fall to the floor one by one. "Oh, looks like they're all numbered." She started arranging them in their proper order, a grid, which ended up covering about ten square feet. The two gazed at the original Industrial Centre blueprint.

"Broooo," said Nuru, squatting down, "there's a fuck ton of shit on this." The map showed a cross section of the building with the aboveground portion of the Industrial Centre taking up only the top ten percent of the blueprint. Descending from the warehouse looked to be something similar to a spinal column mixed with a robotic ant colony. Dozens of tunnels shot off from the Big Deep Hole, which stretched all the way to the bottom row of paper.

The tunnels were shown nonlinear, like a subway map, leading to cutaways of the various rooms in order to conserve space. *Mechanical 1*, *Garage*, *Heat Bank*, and *Shelter* were among some of the room names Nuru found notable.

"This is pretty nuts," said Gwendoline, "but which of these places are the cool ones and which ones are actually what they say they are?" She turned away from the blueprints and flipped through the interactive map on her PC_X, her eyes trying to distinguish a pattern. A moment later she found the Cistern, labeled *Emergency Escape C*. "Oh, I got it I think. Dwaine or someone must've color coded them. I'm guessing all of the non-functional rooms—or at least that are serving a different purpose—are labeled in teal."

"Well I hope you're correct because I don't really want to walk into some random one and be exposed to more radiation. I'm done with that bogus crap for the rest of my life."

"We got kinda lucky Dwaine told us that cold storage was the one where the radioactive stuff is supposed to be. Key word, *supposed*. That makes sense though since it's the furthest away room on here."

"So I'm looking," Nuru said slowly as he squatted, "and I can't determine what's going on at the bottom."

Gwendoline looked up at the physical map. "Looks like what Dwaine said, some sorta thing for making the diamonds that they no longer use. Not sure how that was supposed to work. Look, the real place that's happening is over in this one." She pointed to a larger room full of equipment intertwined with tubing. "I still don't quite understand how this is all put together."

"I don't either and I'll probably never know." Nuru felt

a hunger pang and stood up. "Would it be wrong of me to have a pizza right now?"

"No, not at all," she said, turning again to the map on her PC_X. "He would've put it away if he didn't want us to."

Nuru had already started walking over to the ingredient station. "I'm gonna metaphorically pour one out for Dwaine right now, and by that I mean I'm gonna make two pizzas for myself."

"Actually can you put one in for me as well? There are definitely extra rooms on the digital map that aren't on the physical one."

"There's a note over here," said Nuru, noticing a piece of paper on the counter of the station. "Dear GweNu," Nuru sighed, "please eat up the rest of the shit in here. There's more of some ingredients growing here too but some you'll have to get at the FDC if you wanna keep this stocked. Also, I died because of poisoned lettuce. Just kidding, the lettuce is fine and the kind I have here is amazing on taco pizza." Nuru laughed under his breath. "Wow, this guy never gets old."

"I could actually go for a taco pizza right now if you didn't start making mine already."

Nuru looked at the lettuce. It looked like normal lettuce. "No I didn't, I'll throw one together for you."

She started comparing the digital schematic to the physical blueprint for other inconsistencies. "I guess you never really think of it when you live so close and see it all the time, but there's a lot of high-tech shit going on here. Pretty crazy that one guy was overseeing the whole thing. Although I think we agreed he didn't actually do anything here besides use its resources for dumb shit."

"Yeah, who knows. It's certainly interesting. So you thinking about exploring some of these rooms?" He surveyed the ingredients, not knowing where to begin for his own pizzas.

"The more I look at this though, the more I see that the opulent rooms served more than one function. Seemed like this was also made to be a sustainable closed system for supporting people. Maybe in the case of emergency or war or something. Strange they'd include it so close to a fusion reactor though, but I guess why not."

"There are too many frickin' choices here in the pizza-making station. I can't make up my mind. Do I want 'shrooms and olives? Do I want ground beef and maybe bacon? I wish there was a list of four I could pick so I don't have to use up all this mental energy in my head short-circuiting my brain."

"Just do something easy so you can get my taco one in there, I'm trying to not starve too here."

"Well the thing is, do I really want something easy or do I want to expand my horizons? What would Dwaine want me to do?" Gwendoline didn't answer so he continued, "Alright I'll do a plain cheese, fuck it." He threw it into the still warm oven and tossed a couple more pieces of wood in to get the temperature back up. "So, uh, what do you think about checking out some of the rooms?"

"I don't know, maybe. I'm thinking of continuing looking at these maps, maybe then we eat and assess the situation from there."

"Sounds fine to me." Nuru threw his next pizza in the oven, an amalgamation of ingredients he'd put on, overcompensating for the simplicity of the first. Action on too many ingredient choices may have lead him to failure on his rebound pizza. However, the plain cheese was already showing signs of optimal cooking. He finished part one of the taco pizza and frowned while sliding it into the oven. "I really done goofed, that taco pizza is gonna turn out frickin' dank AF"

Gwendoline didn't respond. After a moment of Nuru expectantly looking at her, she put down her PC_X to inspect the oven's contents. "I don't know how long I wanna stay here if we don't know if we're gonna be able to get back. What I'm thinking is that we hit the garage first and see if there's transport for us and if there is, we make sure it's working and then check out a couple other rooms."

"Seems good," said Nuru, looking into the oven. "Maybe even as good as this pizza is gonna be."

"So weird how the past six months have been boring and quiet as usual and then suddenly we're here again about to eat pizza. Under such a weird circumstance too. Well, not a weird circumstance knowing Dwaine, but still. It's like this is the part after a funeral where everyone eats mini sandwiches, except it's just us and the food is objectively better. Sorta makes you wonder how many different combinations of toppings there are."

Nuru open-mouth frowned as he thought. "I suppose you're right. When someone dies, we all have to drop everything. Now that's actually pretty strange. We gotta scramble for someone who's now frickin' dead? Kinda a scam . . . well I guess not really. I don't know. Plus in this case Dwaine essentially lied to us to get us down here."

"Makes me kinda sad actually," she looked into the oven, "that we were pretty much the only people Dwaine knew or trusted. We were only with him for half a day and then saw him again and I swore at him and called him a prick and shit, which he was. Just kinda sad to think."

"I wonder what he thought we were gonna do with this. Surely he didn't expect us to live here? Isn't there some organization that we gotta alert about his death?"

"I mean probably," Gwendoline took a seat on the floor. "Seems like Dwaine would've told us about that if he wanted us to. You know there's no way he's on good terms with them anymore."

"Yeah, I don't know."

Gwendoline resumed looking at the digital map while getting warmed up by the radiant heat of the oven and Nuru started a self-guided tour of the hangar, inspecting the equipment Dwaine had moved to the side.

"I wonder when he moved all this crap. He must've had a plan in place for a while." Gwendoline didn't respond, lost in the digital map. He trotted to the hangar door and spotted small amounts of wet debris in the pattern of treads. A vehicle must've returned not long ago, ruling out the possibility Dwaine was buried somewhere in the Industrial Centre. The trail of wetness didn't lead to Dwaine's truck, but gently disappeared before it would've hit the wall closest to the Big Deep Hole. He checked on the pizzas and sat near Gwendoline after confirming that they needed a little more time. He chuckled to himself. Funny that for everything there was to see here, he was just sitting cross-legged on the floor waiting for pizzas to cook. He gave them another thirty seconds and took the first one out.

"I think I figured out how to get downstairs to the garage," said Gwendoline. She looked up at Nuru and grinned with a hint of excitement. "It's different than most of the rooms, which you have to somehow go down the hole to get to, not sure how to do that yet."

Nuru mentally recreated the second pizza in his head and took it out so it stayed in as exactly as long as the first had.

"But how do we get down there is the question." Gwendoline spoke slowly. "There should be a button somewhere on the wall on the side of the steps with the hole. According to this, the whole floor—or not the whole floor, but a large portion of the floor—moves to allow large objects to be transported down a couple stories." She shook her head and stared into space. "I don't know how they got all the shit down to these other deep rooms. The garage floors beneath us are their own separate thing compared to those."

Nuru took Gwendoline's pizza out and added fresh lettuce and tomato. "You want any hot sauce or sour cream?"

"Sure, maybe a little sour cream."

He picked up the tube sitting in the ice bath and squeezed it generously onto her pizza.

"What you seein' now?" said Nuru, setting down the pizzas in front of them.

"I'm seeing that unless Dwaine buried himself with a bunch of vehicles, there should be some below us we can use."

"Nice." He took the first bite of his pizza and it scalded the roof of his mouth. "Gah!" He slapped it down and stood up to walk to the sink. "You want water?"

"Yeah sure," said Gwendoline without paying much attention to what she just said yes to.

"So what's the plan on whether or not we're gonna take a look at any of these buildings?" He filled up two cups with water.

"Not sure. There's just a lot of shit going on here. I think honestly it would take us like two days just to visit all of them even just to give 'em a peek."

"I'm sure we could do it in a day." Nuru handed a water cup to Gwendoline.

"Probably, but given that we don't know how the transportation system works, and that Dwaine was talking about the emergency system blasting whole sections out into the sky, I don't wanna rush into that."

"Decent point I s'pose." Nuru tried the pizza again, gingerly this time. It was at a better temperature.

"I think the plan we have right now still is fine. We go down to the garage and see what's popping down there before anything else, then either try and figure out how to use the hole's transportation system or figure out if they're like stairs that fold out or something."

"Maybe a five-mile-long rope ladder."

"You're joking but I wouldn't rule it out." She put down her PC_X getting the map out of her mind before taking a bite of her taco pizza. "Daaamn," she said, chewing with her mouth full, "freakin' good work on this."

"No big deal," said Nuru. "Just something I used to whip up in college."

They ate the rest of their pizza. Nuru struggled to finish his second, not because he was full, but because of his misguided choice of toppings. He got up, playing off his poor choice by groaning and patting his belly. He threw the dishes into the sink and leaned against the ingredient station. "Maybe our next goal should be figuring out how Dwaine died."

"Nah, I don't know how much I give a shit about that to be honest."

"What about trying to figure out where his crypt is."

"That might be a better idea, but I feel like that'll be more fun once summer rolls around and we officially claim his truck as our own. Although we'd have to figure out how to make fuel for it."

"He could've done one of those vegetable oil things."

"Yeah maybe. Or maybe there's a more nondescript vehicle below."

"You know Dwaine would be the type of guy to remove all the official looking decals too."

"Certainly wouldn't put that past him."

Gwendoline investigated where the elevator button was supposed to be. After two scans, she found a panel cut out into the wall which flipped up, revealing a set of numbers from one to five. She pressed *1* on the keypad and a rectangle of red lights lit up designating the edge of the platform where it was about to lower. "Get your ass over onto this," she said to Nuru. He speed-walked from the ingredient station, where he'd started casually eating some shredded cheese, and into the red zone on the floor. The platform didn't move. She hit the keypad again, the lights turned green, and the two started to descend.

CHAPTER TWO

"Yoikes!" said Nuru in a nervous laugh poorly masked by irony as the platform jerked. After they'd lowered about sixty feet, the elevator slowed and came to a gentle halt. Above their heads, a panel the size of the platform previously attached to the ceiling slid forward to fill the hole the elevator left. A door the whole width of the platform glided open revealing a room identical to Dwaine's former workshop. Gwendoline burst out laughing.

"No fucking way," said Nuru, shaking his head aggressively.

The garage was completely full of Dwaine's belongings that used to be on the floor above. The couch, cabinetry, and skeletons of other projects were scattered about together with other previously unseen items. "We don't even need to see this." Gwendoline hit 2 twice on the elevator keypad and they felt their stomachs enter their mouths as the elevator moved downward at a quicker pace. When it slowed, the two felt an excitement anticipating something novel, but Garage 2 was empty.

"I'm gonna be honest, I was not expecting this," said Nuru. "Not even like a helicopter or something?"

"Typical Dwaine," said Gwendoline, hitting the button for Garage 3. It too was empty.

"Maybe each of the crew had their own garage?" said Nuru as they lowered. "I can't remember how many people Dwaine said worked here though."

"Kinda weird if you ask me, but I guess what do you really need at a place like this? There's a lot of storage for something that's self-sufficient." Garage 4 was empty.

"All right, for all the marbles now." Nuru rubbed his hands together, grinning, and pressed the button for Garage 5. The elevator dropped downward in what felt like twice the distance in the same amount of time. Gwendoline glanced at Nuru who, even though it was dark, was able to see his face, contorted in anticipation for something spectacular. The elevator slowed and Nuru's heart sped up. "I don't know why I'm getting excited for this but there's gotta be something cool in the lowest garage."

The elevator stopped and the door opened. "Awww yeah." His positivity sounded scripted, masking minor disappointment with what he saw. Parked nearest the elevator was an aircraft that looked too big to fit on the elevator platform. It looked higher tech than standard passenger planes, but also looked as if Dwaine's last activity with it was flying through a mud storm. Behind the aircraft sat a fleet of snow machines, half open-air, half enclosed. Behind them, a row of four-wheelers, and behind those were two sedans and three trucks. Every single vehicle was painted white.

"What the fuck did Dwaine do to this frickin' plane?" said Gwendoline, walking to inspect one of its engines, "It looks like it got thrown through a waterspout that was hugging the shore of a lake or some shit."

"I don't know, but I'm gonna be sittin' pretty rolling up in one of these covered snow machines."

Gwendoline rolled the ladder over to look into the cockpit. "God it's a fuckin' mess in the inside of this too, if that comes as any surprise. I wonder what kinda training it takes to fly one of these."

"Dwaine didn't leave us instructions for that did he?" said Nuru as he sat down on one of the open-air snow machines. He cocked a smile.

"If he wanted us to fly it, I think he would've cleaned it out more. Frickin' sheesh." She hopped down and surveyed the trucks. "These are alright. I think you're right in that we're best suited to take two of those back." She motioned to the enclosed snow machines, "Well should we take two up and then see if we can't get in a visit to one of the 'cool' rooms? What time is it anyway?"

"I dunno, what time did we leave again?" He didn't feel

like digging his PC_X out from his pocket to check so he pretended to forget that was an option.

"It was around thirteen or fourteen I think. Then it took us an hour to get here, and we've been here, what a half-hour or less? Maybe like sixteen-ish?"

"That sounds about right. Maybe not accounting for pizza making time though."

Nuru hopped off the open-air snow machine and headed to the nearest enclosed one. "Do these even have keys or do they just fire up?" he said before flipping the *On* button he spotted. It sprang to life. "Looks like they just fire up." He closed the door, navigated around the aircraft, and parked on the elevator platform; Gwendoline was still eyeing the trucks.

"Would it be wrong of me to take one of these instead?" She was on the other side of the room and didn't seem to be talking to anyone in particular.

"What?" said Nuru, cutting the engine.

"Yeah probably." She jumped out of the truck bed and drove a snow machine onto the platform.

"Anything else we need to do down here?" asked Nuru. He glanced over at the airplane, still wondering how it had acquired so much mud.

"Eh, I don't know. What are your thoughts? Seems like a fairly non-quirky room."

"I wonder which vehicle Dwaine used to transport himself to his crypt. Kinda hard to tell since none of these vehicles are clean and everything's already dried."

"What did he use to transport all the cement blocks?" said Gwendoline, realizing the answer as she spoke. "I was half expecting there to be some sort of heavy equipment down here but he must've used that truck up there."

"Wasn't that what it sounded like he was gonna do? He was talking about installing a crane lift type deal like the kind at shipyards."

"Yeah that's right, good point," said Gwendoline. "Well I guess we should bring these up. Not sure what else is worth doing down here." She hit the 0 button twice and the door slid shut, beginning their ascent.

Back on the first floor, Nuru was ready to keep exploring in spirit, but his body felt tired; the pizza oven was losing heat too. Gwendoline was starting to feel the same way so they decided to return home for the evening and continue to survey the maps from there. Nuru consolidated the pizza ingredients into a tub as Gwendoline started gearing up. When he was ready, she hit the button on the wall, opening the giant hangar door. They pulled forward, and for a second, it looked like the door wouldn't close, but it eventually sensed they'd left and shut behind them. The dark ride back was uneventful apart from something unnerving that popped into Gwendoline's head. Maybe it was the hum of the engine that triggered it, maybe it was her brain's gears still turning but her too exhausted to fuel their spin, but she realized she couldn't remember the events of almost every single day since the summer leading up to the present. It was as if a group of little green men had descended from the sky and abducted her for medical tests before wiping her brain. She'd been active every day since then, mostly working on visual art pieces, but couldn't differentiate a single day, or moment, from the rest. It troubled her.

At the livingspace Gwendoline added Nuru to her previously internal dialog. "How much do you remember of the fall?"

"What do you mean, like what did we do?"

"Yeah, like what specifically do you remember?"

"I remember going to the beach ball-lawn bowling event and coming in third." He took off his jacket and sat down on the couch, still with his boots on. "When I spilled all those oats and a metric ton of them went under the stove; also when I admitted to my mom that I got radiation poisoning by accident. I guess those are the highlights." He snapped out of his trance and started taking off his boots.

Gwendoline rolled her eyes into her head, straining them to get a glimpse of her eyebrows. She took some time before speaking. "It seems like we only remember the things that are anomalous in our lives. I mean, it seems like I should remember making brush strokes, something that I enjoy doing, but I literally don't even remember anything about making that," she said, signaling to the completed painting on the wall. "Like what the shit, brain?"

"I don't know, seems kinda normal." He put his boots into the boot area. "Do we really need to remember the events we repeat day after day? Do I really need to know that I had toast in the morning of X day?"

"Well, I don't know, that isn't really what I meant, I'm talking about like on a bigger picture." She sat down on the couch. "I can look back at my life and say that I made this painting or whatever, but I can't remember the process of making it. Seems like I should, I fuckin' worked on it for like four months straight but I can't remember a single day of it? I remember almost every moment of when we went to the Industrial Centre and met Dwaine—rest in peace—though." She put her legs up on one of the armrests and lay down. "Why should like a week or two take up so much real estate in my head?"

"I don't frickin' know." Nuru smiled; it seemed like Gwendoline was back in one of her modes. He deposited the pizza toppings in the fridge and sat on the kitchen counter. "Perhaps your life didn't progress while you were working on the piece of art. Perhaps the art you created was the culmination of your work alive, like a jellyfish collecting jelly and then using the jelly to make a sandwich. That may not be the perfect example, but whatever." He thought for a moment. "Maybe a 'brain dump' is a better way. Your art is the culmination of your experience alive but the actual process of turning your experience into a tangible good is unremarkable."

"That would, in theory, suggest that the creation of art should only be done at increments of life, after certain experiences, like checkpoints? Then, if you spent your whole life working on art, never going outside, then your art would reflect that? Interesting . . . well, uninteresting."

"Seems fine enough to me. The dude who spends all his time making pictures of dogs is essentially—actually I don't wanna shit on people who do that, for them it's a hobby, they may manifest their life experience in other ways . . ." Nuru lifted himself on his hands from his sitting position and scooched closer to the sink.

"Good point, not everyone is in it for the same reason, but I'd hope that the dude drawing all the dogs is doing something interesting with his time. I don't know. Seems like he'd just really like dogs and all he'd want to talk about is dogs."

Nuru picked himself up again and slid into the sink; it was just deep enough to where his knees could bend over the edge. "You'll probably remember me doing this," he said, casually kicking his legs up and down.

"Yeah probably." She didn't think she actually would. "But you're saying that anything created by a person—that they may not remember the process of making—is more or less a self-portrait of their thoughts."

"Yeah, and I guess some people just really, really like dogs," said Nuru. He was finding it somewhat difficult to breathe while his legs were so close to his chest.

"Nothing wrong with that. I just wonder at what point does the process of creation define who you are and should you let it? Is that a rut you should avoid falling into? Maybe what I'm getting at, is that art is just a way to see a truer reflection of who you are. And maybe if all you do is make it—or, therefore, make the same thing over and over—then you'll come to define yourself through your creations. Which may be fine, but probably should just supplement your life, because if you define yourself by the act of creation, your actions will be empty, a bad feedback loop."

"Eh, I think you're onto something there but maybe only halfway." He put his hands out on either side of the sink and lifted himself out.

"So in summary then, I don't remember any of the work I do because it's not worth remembering, but within the work are my thoughts and memories of what *is* worth remembering. I guess I can live with that for now."

"But avast, ye young thinker," Nuru turned around, exposing his now wet pants to Gwendoline, "there is ye problem with ye theory and it is thyne, what about people who work and do the same thing every day? Why can't I remember emptying the same trash can every day for ten years? Why can't I remember checking the water pressure for your house? Or, why can't I remember any of our walks?"

"Well, I think the walks are almost like mini manifestations of our lives then. That can be pretty easily incorporated into the theory. However, for the people who empty the same trash can every day, that I'm having trouble incorporating."

Nuru sat down on the counter with a towel so his pants would dry. "You could say that emptying the same trash is the manifestation of who you are, but that's depressing. I think it's a routine task that your brain forgets about. It *is* part of who you are though. I'd have to think more about that as well."

Gwendoline started speaking just as Nuru finished, "I think maybe any time like that—emptying the same trash—is just like a mini walk. You don't remember it because you were thinking of something else. Painting is all muscle memory, same with dumping a trash into a bigger trash. It's more time for thinking. You use that time to think about other things—other experiences—and some people have more time to think than have time to experience. Maybe that's the key."

"I guess that makes sense. Wait, but then is dumping the trash a self-portrait or a manifestation of experience?" Nuru got up and checked his pants. They were dry enough for him to sit on normal furniture. He sat on the floor near the couch so he could look at Gwendoline as she lounged.

Gwendoline ignored his last thought. "The key is to figure out the balance between the luxury of thought and the luxury of experience then. You don't need to physically manifest your experiences into some sort of artistic object, but maybe you need enough time to decompress them and add them to who you are, sort through them, like those computers that used to unfold proteins—successfully integrating experiences into your life. Having too much time to unfold those proteins and running out of proteins to unfold—or emptying the trash every day—will make you go crazy or feel like crap because you can't think about anything if you don't have other experiences. On the other hand, if all you do is dick around going on cruises and shit, maybe you'll get lost in yourself and your experiences. You'll become some sorta experience bot."

"I don't know, seems like it would be hard to do that."

"Well maybe it's not a fifty-fifty split, but I bet that more people spend their time doing forgettable things, so they're all biased from that perspective. I don't know anyone who's experienced things too much though."

"Who knows what the upper limit of that would be. I think there'd be some severe burnout though. That seems nearly impossible." Nuru started to feel tired at the thought of burnout and lay back on the floor.

"I think if you're some experience fiend, you're really just optimizing experience and forgettableness time; a person like that would still have downtime. All world travelers have downtime. What's a better example is someone who has the experience of constantly playing chess and having to think constantly."

"Yeah, I don't know," said Nuru. "I gotta get up off of this floor before I fall asleep though." He dragged himself onto the wooden straight-backed chair near him. "This is more like it."

"Anyway," Gwendoline sighed, "what are we doing about the Industrial Centre shit? You think we gotta tell the mayor or like contact some NGO about it? Who the shit oversees that?"

"Honestly I don't know," said Nuru, feeling his sleepiness disappear as he sat uncomfortably in the chair, "but obviously I know that you know that I don't know."

"What if this is some indie power plant lost to time. There's gotta be some sort of oversight. But at the same time, maybe not. There are other places like it as far as atmospheric regulation is concerned, so maybe this is low priority for whoever runs this."

"Maybe the group is dissolved. Like what group would put fricking Dwaine in charge, or at least let him be the only one out there?"

"Who knows," said Gwendoline. "Maybe he was better when he was younger."

"There's gotta be someone who needs to be informed about his passing. There's a giantass fusion reactor there, seems like someone needs to be advised of that."

"You'd think." Blood rushed from Gwendoline's head as she got up to use her personal computer. "Maybe tomorrow we can go back and look at his contact list or something, or talk to the mayor. I'm not sure if I want to get him involved though. You're still up for checking out some of those rooms tomorrow, right?"

Nuru gave an affirmative nod. "That'll be weird seeing all that shit. Seems like we're forced to do a bunch of administrative tasks for Dwaine too."

"Yeah, we represent his estate now. How generous of him."

"Some people's kids, man," said Nuru, shaking his head.

"I know, right?" Gwendoline opened up the digital maps of the Industrial Centre to see if she could find any contact information or at least an agency the Industrial Center belonged to. "Maybe straight up they got all this funding independently and were not beholden to any group." She couldn't find any contact information at all on the map. "You'd think there'd be some sort of regulatory group that would come in and inspect it at least occasionally."

"Knowing Dwaine, he was probably a part of whatever regulatory body there was," said Nuru. He went over to his personal computer, "I wonder if there's anything about that in the Archive."

"How much you wanna bet that we'll call some place and they'll tell us something like, 'Everything is electronically monitored and we'll send someone out to fix it as needed' or something bogus like that. I mean I guess the whole place is probably fail-safe, but having someone on hand seems smart."

"Well, what are they gonna do in the case of a meltdown? Send in a bunch of people?" Nuru executed an Archive search hoping to find a group to contact. The results looked daunting and he gave up.

"Good point, but what about preventing a meltdown? A switch could fail to flip, no one is there to flip it. . . ."

"You think you can search for this stuff? I don't think I can handle it," he said, slumping." Dwaine said something about that bot that checked for radiation. I bet that there're other bots that can do that shit."

Gwendoline frowned. "Yeah probably, but that seems dangerous. Those could fail too. Lots of stuff could fail. It just seems weird that there's something so potentially dangerous completely unmanned."

"Let's be real here though, it's probably actually safer now that Dwaine's dead than when he was alive. He was obviously doing a lot of unsafe shit in there."

"Good point. Maybe this isn't the end of the world if we don't alert someone right away."

"I agree. I think we have some time to see the place before taking action."

"Still, I think we can both agree that it's an odd situation."

"For sure."

Gwendoline spent the rest of the night looking up information about the Industrial Centre and various other air capture and fusion projects, making note of figureheads and hoping Dwaine would have at least one on his contact list.

CHAPTER THREE

The next day resembled the previous day: it was as dark when the two woke up as it was when they went to sleep. Nuru made himself some warm water and waited for Gwendoline to rise. She'd stayed up an hour later. He sipped his warm water and moseyed to Gwendoline's personal computer. Next to the input device was a notepad with a short list of names and titles, presumably people worth notifying. He sat down at his own personal computer; the last thing he'd done before going to bed was look at information about eucalyptus trees, hardly helping the cause. Comforted knowing Gwendoline had found the information they needed, he dug in deeper to the world of eucalyptus, continuing to read about how it fit into Earth's ecosystem.

Gwendoline got up a half hour later and was fully lucid, a trait Nuru never figured out how she acquired. "I compiled a list of people that we could call and let know about Dwaine's death. I hope to God that one of these people is on Dwaine's contact list. Seems like there was a lot of turnover at a lot of these places and it seems like most groups no longer exist. But, I'd be surprised if Dwaine wasn't in contact with one of the contemporary regulatory bodies."

"Eucalyptus leaves used to be the staple diet of the koala."

"Yeah, I know," said Gwendoline, already putting on her outdoor gear. "You ready to take off out there?"

"You're not gonna eat anything first?" said Nuru, trying to bide time for himself to eat.

"No, not super hungry right now. I'm sure we'll find where Dwaine was storing his other food. Also we have all those pizza toppings we could bring back with us."

"Well if you don't mind, I might have a li'l somethin' somethin' before we depart."

Gwendoline gave Nuru some side-eye, "Well, eat like the wind because I wanna get all this administrative B.S. out of the way."

"Sheesh, I'll just make myself a salad from that toppings tub." He took the container out of the fridge, causing a bottle of salsa and some almond milk to topple out. "How the crap did I even get this in here last night anyway?" Gwendoline exhaled slowly as she stood fully dressed in her outdoor gear watching Nuru eat. Eventually he finished and put the tub back in the fridge, finally suiting up to Gwendoline's relief.

"Sure looks a lot more like night than it does morning!" he said as he stepped outside. Gwendoline didn't respond. Nuru'd said that line almost every day since it got dark, and from day one, chose not to elicit any emotional response. Their snow machines turned over first try and they rode through the darkness to the Industrial Centre.

This time, they entered through the large hangar door, momentarily having trouble getting it open. They parked their snow machines behind Dwaine's truck.

"Alright so where is Dwaine's personal computer?" said Gwendoline, looking around.

"My guess is he moved it back down to the garage he was using," he said as he took off his jacket.

"That's a pretty darn good guess since it doesn't appear to be here." She eyed the pizza oven, "Kinda sad seeing that not in operation. This place feels a little less homey."

"It wasn't that homey to begin with, but I agree." He joined Gwendoline near the oven. "It did improve the atmosphere of the space."

She pivoted on her heels and strolled to the elevator platform. Nuru followed and they lowered into the ground. The two waded through Dwaine's belongings as if looking for a missing person until Gwendoline spotted the computer near the far wall. "What are the odds that Dwaine has security protection on this?" she said as they circled in.

"I'd say there's about a zero percent chance. Zero point zero at the most."

Indeed, his personal computer had no security features and Gwendoline was able to access all his files after waking up the machine. "Makes you wonder why he encrypted that drive he gave us," said Nuru.

"Maybe he doesn't have the map on this computer. But also, that was a pretty crappy password anyway." She pulled up his contact list and compared it to the names on her notes. "Wow, looks like every single person I have written down is on here."

"A man with copious amounts of social capital."

"Too bad you can't take that with you when you die." She flipped between contacts on the screen in an impatient fidget. "Although, it still has value to us now." She glanced at Nuru, "So who do we call first?"

"I suppose whoever has the coolest job title." He looked at Gwendoline's list. "Maybe Patricia Pishchalnikova—or however you say it—chair of the HyperFusion Research Project and co-founder of the Arctic Clean Air Regulatory Board."

"Yeah that's who I'm thinking too." She expanded her contact information. Looks like she's a bit younger than Dwaine, in her mid-forties. I'm just gonna go ahead and say that there's a fifty percent chance Patricia and he didn't get along, and a fifty percent chance they were indifferent to each other."

"What time is it in Yakutsk right now though?" said Nuru. "Oh wait never mind it says the local time right below, LOL at my swag."

Gwendoline hovered over the call button. "You think it's too early to call over there?"

Nuru shrugged. "Eh, actually who gives a fuck, it's frickin' darkness there too and getting a call at like five probably means a higher chance of her actually picking up."

Gwendoline raised her eyebrows and hit call. After half a ring, a woman's voice speaking in Russian materialized. Nuru turned to Gwendoline with an *oh crap, what do we do?* expression, but Gwendoline remained calm.

"Hi, do you speak English? We're trying to reach Patricia. This is Gwendoline calling from the Industrial Centre from Dwaine's personal computer."

The voice switched to English, completely dropping the Russian accent, "Oh, hi Gwendoline! This is she. What's going on there?" She sounded calm and not the slightest bit perturbed at the early morning call.

"Everything's fine—for starters—but we were just checking in to see if you were aware of what's happened here in the past two days."

"I'm confused as to what you mean," said Patricia.

"Well," Gwendoline looked at Nuru with her eyebrows expectantly raised, not knowing how to proceed, "Dwaine died yesterday and as far as we know, didn't tell anyone. It sounded to me like he was putting me in charge of doing that."

"Oh I'm sorry to hear that! Dwaine was a very bright man and his work inspired my own. I'm very sorry to hear that he passed away."

"Yeah," she glanced at Nuru, "but I was just wondering if anything needed to be done. As far as oversight or letting the right people know . . ."

"Sure, thanks for calling. I can pass that information along. Let me open up the files on the Industrial Centre." She paused for a moment. "It looks like you and a person named Nuru are both listed as the maintainers of the location. Is that correct?"

"Uh, well the thing is, we don't know anything about maintaining this place and have only been here a total of three times. I think we were the only young people that Dwaine knew."

"Hmm, I'm looking at all the readouts from the reactor

and HyperFrost system and their history has been perfect every day since they were put into operation. The odds of the two of you having to do anything are quite small."

"I'm not sure if that gives me any confidence that we should be the new maintainers of the facility."

It sounded to them like the voice on the other end laughed but it was hard to tell. "Don't worry about it. The system was made to run without oversight for at least two hundred years; the chances of you needing to do something are quite small."

"But in the case of an emergency, don't you want someone who knows what they're doing?"

"If Dwaine picked you then he knew you could handle it. And again, it's more of a formality. In the event of a meltdown—which won't happen—the whole facility locks down and closes off from the rest of the world. It's better to be away from it when that happens. Maintainer activities mostly involve hosing off the building every once in a while."

Gwendoline shook her head and sighed. "Well, okay I guess. There isn't some sort of plan where a response team flies in from somewhere?"

"There is such a plan, but it involves evacuating everyone."

"Okay." Gwendoline didn't know what to say next and waited for Patricia to speak again.

"Do you have any other questions?"

"Uh, I guess not. Things are just gonna keep happening here then? Nothing is changing?"

"Nothing will be changing."

"Okay I guess," said Gwendoline, "I'm sorry to have woken you up."

"Oh, ha! I'm not in Yakutsk right now. I'm at Base Four—in former Greenland!"

"Oh ok, well I'm sorry to have bothered you."

"Not a problem, if you have any other issues, you can call me at any time. Add my information to your contacts as well so you can call from your PC_X if need be, I don't foresee you having any problems."

"Ok, thanks, bye!"

"Ciao!"

She hit the keyboard, ending the call. "Well that was certainly something else."

"So where do we go from here?" He stepped back and leaned against what appeared to be a stack of rusty brake drums half-covered in lacquer.

"Maybe check out some of the other places down the hole I guess."

"Did you figure out how we're supposed to navigate that stuff?"

Gwendoline shook her head, "No, never did, was focused more on getting a list of people together."

"Hmm. I guess we figure out how to do that then? Some part of me doesn't have motivation to explore here though, weirdly. Not sure why."

"Yeah I don't know. It's like now it's just a bunch of rooms. The lack of Dwaine or a personality maybe makes it less cool. Plus it's not like we're being edgelords and tres- passing."

"Decidedly less cool." He pushed off the brake drums and waded over to a table with a beaker on top and squinted at the blue liquid inside. It smelled like singed rubber and metal shavings. "It's not that I want to *not* check the place out, but I feel like there's no rush to do it now."

"Yeah I know what you mean. No reason to apart from finding all these luxury rooms. Honestly though, I'd feel bad using all this shit. There's no reason that we should be entitled to use the shit here. I don't deserve to take a mineral bath in the cistern any more than you deserve it or your dad deserves it."

"My dad does *not* deserve to take a mineral bath here."

Gwendoline joined Nuru at the table, brushing away empty glassware and sitting down on top. "So do we now initiate plan *after someone dies we turn their place of residence into a museum* or is that even allowed? For all we know that could be against whatever that governing body Patricia was a part of."

"It would rest my conscience knowing only the two of us could legally use the mineral baths," said Nuru. He touched the side of the beaker filled with the blue liquid, finding it a bit warm.

Gwendoline's brows furrowed as she watched his finger smudge the glass. "Yes, yes, I agree."

"It's weird being surrounded by all this junk—for lack of a better word. It's like we're inside one of those living fossils," he said, putting air quotes around the last two words.

She hopped off the table to pace back and forth, but finding no room, sat back down. Her eyes stared through the underground walls into space, imagining her stare penetrated everything like neutrinos passing through objects. She hopped down again, this time to lean against the table. "Things seem to be getting more non-linear, our paths have become like the end of the water slide." She paused to continue staring into space. "Maybe water slide isn't the right example, maybe something more like a field of grass that you're not sure if you have to mow today but you'll have to mow it at some point in the next week but you freeze up before hopping on the mower because there are too many different ways you could attack the grass."

"I don't think the people who regularly mow grass think about that."

"Maybe you're correct. Maybe it's your first time mowing a certain area. But maybe our situation is more like an opportunity to stop and think about shit or something."

"Could be."

"Like we could move all our shit out here and become even more reclusive than we already are. We could explore some of the buildings. We could never come here again and not tell anyone that Dwaine died."

"So many options . . ." he said, sounding a little flippant.

"Thank you all previous humans that existed for these opportunities, I guess."

"Let's pour one out." He started lifting up the beaker acting like he was going to drip some on the floor.

"We're so young," Gwendoline was in a trance and didn't notice Nuru's joke or his treating of this topic with little care. "The world is ours, in a way." She sat back on the table and stayed looking off at nothing for another minute before speaking again. "It would be wrong to call Patricia back and ask if we can have other people in here for tours, wouldn't it?" She hopped down again, forgetting that there wasn't room to pace.

"Well, I don't think she'd mind actually, but I don't know if you wanna develop a rapport based on calling her all the time."

"There could be some sense to your words, Nuru." She sat up on the table for the nth time after running into the same pacing obstacles.

Nuru was ready to change the subject and Gwendoline must've felt it, even in her trance-like state. She slid off the table and made her way to the elevator without speaking. Nuru followed. A moment later they were back at ground level.

"I'm thinking we continue the plan we had before I got sidetracked," said Gwendoline. She pulled out her PC_X and started looking for navigation instructions for the other rooms within the building. Nuru left her to it, deciding to take a look down the Big Deep Hole. There was nothing but blackness, no anomalies within its curved walls, yet according to what they knew, it was the only way to many of the rooms. Maybe there were doors further down, but none were visible.

"I think I figured out how the transport system works," said Gwendoline standing up to meet Nuru at the hole, "if you can believe this, which I'm sure you can," she pointed up to the bars suspended above the hole near the ceiling, "there should be an elevator system that goes up and down the hole. The problem is, obviously there's no sign of an elevator. It looks like at some point Dwaine took it off, probably scavenging parts."

"I can believe that," said Nuru, "So then how do we navigate?"

"That's a good question." She peered into the darkness momentarily. "I was wondering if there was a fail-safe measure in place for that, but honestly I don't think there is. Well, there's no way down without the elevator, but there are ways out if you're already down. A couple of the rooms seem to *actually* be 'escape passageways', which you can get to even if the elevator fails. If there was a melt-down—or the elevator broke—people would go from the room they're in to the nearest exit room, which would always be below them. Humans are technically allowed in the cold storage room—the bottommost room of the hole—so if you're down there trying to kill yourself you'd be screwed anyway. The point is, there's some sort of zip line to get people to the nearest exit. I'm just spitballin' but that seems how it works."

"So how do we get down there then? Rebuild the elevator?"

"Yeah, pretty much. Either that or rappel down."

Nuru smiled ironically, "Ah, that sounds fun. A nice way to spend the morning. So then how far down is the nearest room?"

"The nearest room down there is marked as 'Piping Hub' which is apparently an area where a bunch of pipes meet for easier access or something. It's a half mile down and also is noted for containing hazardous materials."

Nuru did an empty spit-take. "And it's not listed as one of the cool rooms?"

"Not according to this. The closest 'cool room'—the Pressure Room—is further down from the Piping Hub by about a quarter mile."

"Christ, so the first cool room is almost a mile down the hole." Nuru frowned and looked down the BDH. "So then to get out, we'd have to use an emergency system—that we don't even know works—and go down further."

"Well that's only in the situation where we couldn't climb back up to the top because of a fire or something. We can always climb up assuming we rappelled all the way down. Maybe we could even outfit Dwaine's truck with a towing mechanism so we could get pulled up."

Nuru was still frowning; it was starting to hurt his face.

"This is above my pay grade. My pay grade is like, making pizzas, and that's too much. Are there any other places like the cistern that are near the surface of the ground?"

"Yeah, I think there are. There are three of those total. The other two are just as far away by land as the cistern was. We'd have to take snow machines out there for sure. Probably shovels to dig 'em out. Might be difficult, but doable."

Nuru leaned against the guardrails. "Why the hell did Dwaine remove the elevator?"

"No idea."

"Do we know it's actually disassembled, or could it be somewhere else?"

"Not sure, I guess it could be in with all of Dwaine's stuff, but I think we would've noticed something that looks like a giant elevator capsule."

"What the heck is that guy's problem?" Nuru shook his head in disbelief. "What would cause a man to remove the elevator?"

"I know that's rhetorical, but the whole place is autonomous so there was no need for anyone to use the elevator. He probably wasn't doing anything with radioactive materials, or maybe they have their own way of ending up in cold storage."

Nuru stuck his lips together tightly and looked up at the cage that used to support the elevator. "Couldn't he have fabricated his own parts if he needed an elevator?"

"Maybe. The more I think about it, the more I wonder if he was after the cabling. That's something that would be hard to make. Maybe he needed a bunch of it for the tow hitch on his truck."

"Wouldn't surprise me at this point."

Gwendoline strode back to the hangar area and sat on the floor. She was at a loss but this time didn't enter a liquidy state of philosophy, instead she looked at the problem pragmatically. There wasn't going to be a way for them to get the elevator working, and she didn't fancy a trip to the other rooms while it was still cold and dark, and Nuru wouldn't either. There was little they could do except go back to their livingspace and consider letting the mayor know about Dwaine's death. Maybe gauge his interest in making the Industrial Centre tourable too, or at least connect them with someone who could fix the elevator. There was nothing they could do here anymore.

"Well, should be blow this joint?" she said.

"What?" Nuru was still looking into the Big Deep Hole.

"Should we get out of here?" she said, louder.

"You don't wanna go and check out either of the undiscovered rooms?"

"Do you?"

"Well not really, but I'd go with you if you wanted to."

"I was thinking that those can wait until it's brighter out and there's less snow over everything."

"I think that's a totally fair call," said Nuru. He pushed off from the guardrail and started for the snow machines.

"You can't see another way we could check out the rooms here given the tools available to us, can you?"

"Not really, but also I don't think I'd know how to operate a chainsaw if someone asked me to."

"Well I wouldn't either since no one needs chainsaws since there aren't any trees, but I guess that's besides the point."

"I suppose we should get out of here then."

Nuru climbed into his snow machine and flipped it

around facing the exit, waiting for Gwendoline to finish her last round of thoughts, and the two departed.

CHAPTER FOUR

It was about noon when they returned to their living-space. Something had changed in the heating system and the room felt ten degrees colder than when they departed. Still in his outdoor gear, Nuru cranked the thermostat, tracking snow into the kitchen area.

"I thought about something during the ride back," said Gwendoline, refraining from taking off her outdoor gear.

"Oh?" Nuru's eyebrows jumped as he started kicking off his boots in front of the fridge, mainly due to him remembering he had some apples that needed to be eaten.

"Yeah, I thought that there could've been some sort of deeper meaning about Dwaine taking the elevator out and I arrived at the conclusion that he probably took the elevator out for the same reason we suggested earlier, that he needed parts for the winch on the truck and related things."

"So you've eliminated all other variables then? No mystery there?" He pulled an apple from behind the pizza toppings tub and started eating it.

"No other variables. What I think we do now is go talk to the mayor and ask how feasible turning the Industrial Centre into a museum is and then he'll tell us that it's not feasible and that the only way we're going to fix the elevator is if we get someone like your dad and his colleagues to fix it, but that's not possible because they're not gonna be able to source some of the materials for it. Well, they might be able to, but I'll bet Dwaine cut a lot of the cabling down which would have to be put back together, which may not be possible. And all that's assuming that we'll be able to find all of the cabling. I think the main reason we visit the mayor is to tell him that Dwaine died, although maybe he doesn't even care about that either."

"I'm not sure if he would or not." Nuru was enjoying his snack but the cold temperature in the livingspace combined with its prior refrigeration was making him colder than he was outside.

"I don't fully understand Anik."

Nuru leaned against the counter and folded his arms, apple residue getting on his jacket. "I think it's clear that he's generally unhappy, but I can't tell if that's how he actually normally is or not."

"I don't know, but I'm thinking of heading over to his house right now. You interested in going?"

"Well yeah I'm interested in going, why did you let me start taking off all my shit if we were gonna be going right back outside?"

She pressed her lips together annoyed by his lack of observational skills. "I was distracted by something else."

"I see." Nuru frowned before taking another bite of his apple and went to the door, taking three more bites and throwing it into the compost. He zipped up his coat and attached his choppers to his sleeves. Gwendoline watched in silence. She was relieved when they departed as she was starting to get uncomfortably warm.

It was motionless outside so they didn't need their hoods and could talk to each other without having to raise their voices. They set their course for the mayor's house, both silently assuming he wouldn't be at his office.

"I don't think I'd ever known fruit to make me cold before."

"I'm sorry to hear that. Sometimes that stuff can happen."

A warm light emanated through the windows of Anik's house tipping them off that he was home.

"I'm excited to see Louis again," said Gwendoline, knocking on the door.

"Yeah me too. I hope he's in good spirits."

The door opened about a second after he'd finished speaking. Nuru internally frowned, wondering if the mayor had been spying out the window or if he was already standing close to the door in anticipation of new arrivals. His internal frown lasted only a split second before changing to an external smile as Anik's face appeared at the door with Louis bounding toward them.

"Hi, Anik!" said Gwendoline. "We come bearing news which you may or may not be interested in."

Anik smiled at them. He hadn't had guests since they'd last been there, if you could call caretakers guests.

"How are you guys doing?" He stepped back to allow them in, forcing Louis to awkwardly backpedal.

"Oh, we're doing alright," said Nuru. "Just out enjoying the weather."

"It's actually not too bad out today," said Gwendoline, turning Nuru's throwaway statement into an earnest one she felt would appeal more to their host.

"Yeah, according to the thermometer it's four degrees warmer than yesterday," said Anik. "Please take your stuff off, I was about to make some food for myself. Do you two want anything? Well, I'm less making food for myself and more preparing to eat pre-prepared food, but I'm still happy to share."

"What's on the skillet this afternoon?" said Nuru, trying his best to sound cheery and indifferent about himself consuming food and instead appear interested in what the mayor was going to be eating.

"I was going to have some peanut butter toast with the homemade bread that Sherry makes."

"Oooh, that's hard to resist, that bread is really good." Nuru's facial expression looked like he'd just been shot in the stomach and Anik couldn't tell for certain, but rightly moved to the toaster assuming Nuru would eat as many pieces as he could supply.

"I'll put you down for a couple pieces then," he said.

"Oh, I suppose so."

"Take your stuff off too, don't be shy! You can leave it all by the door there." The mayor sidestepped two more paces, arriving at the toaster portion of the kitchen area and started putting bread into the toaster. Anik's departure allowed Louis to finally greet the pair after patiently waiting for attention to turn to him.

"How are you today, Mr. Louis?" said Gwendoline. She squatted down and rubbed both sides of his muzzle which brought Louis great joy. Louis was doing well today and had spent most of the time relaxing near the heater. Gwendoline stood up to take off her gear and allow Nuru dog access. He patted the friendly creature on the head.

"You're looking awfully chipper today, sir," Nuru said to the dog, "I hope you've been able to get enough sleep the past couple months." Louis had, in fact, been able to get enough sleep, but there was always more sleeping to be done.

"I'm sorry I still don't have enough chairs, so one of you will have to stand or sit on the floor."

"Oh that's fine," said Gwendoline. "Someone's got to keep Mr. Louis company down here."

"I'll need to sit too if I'll be eating toast so that works out about perfectly," said Nuru. He sat down in the *non-Anik* chair and Gwendoline sat on the floor, creating a conversation triangle. Louis was excited that she was joining him on the floor, clambering over to her and knocking her down.

Anik had a premonition more bad news was on the way so he silently continued preparing food, letting them bring it up. As much as he liked seeing the two, it seemed they always came bearing bad news. He didn't have to wait long. As soon as Gwendoline got her torso upright after being knocked over, she started talking.

"Yesterday afternoon Dwaine sent me a message saying he was gonna kill himself because he had an unrecoverable illness."

Anik remained silent. To Gwendoline and Nuru, he seemed more or less indifferent about Dwaine, but he was more or less indifferent about everyone.

"Regardless about that," she continued, "he told all regulatory agencies and stakeholders of the Industrial Centre that the two of us are the new overseers of the facility."

Anik frowned for a split second before his cheeks rose, his body eager to take up a new problem to distract from his own. "Why would he do that?" he said, already knowing the correct answer.

"Mainly because he's Dwaine and he's lazy is my guess," said Nuru.

Anik smelled that the toast was almost ready. "So what does that mean for you two?"

"Well, mostly it means that we get in trouble if something goes wrong, but we called Patrica and told her that we didn't know what the hell we were doing—she's the head of two things that I don't remember the name of—and she didn't seem to be worried."

"Interesting." Anik brought two pieces of toast with generous amounts of peanut butter to Nuru. He got a plate for himself and sat down. The QuadSlot hyper-efficient toaster he went lengths to get was finally paying off. That made him feel okay.

"So therefore, if what Dwaine once told us is true—that he wished the diamonds could be a tourist attraction—the two of us may now be mirroring his words in a different hue. We've looked at the digital maps of the Industrial Center and tracked down all of the areas that have weird vanity type shit in them and were thinking of opening those rooms up to the public as like a museum thing, or maybe like an interactive thing. People could use the Industrial Centre's mineral bath, for example."

Anik laughed. "You think people are going to go two miles out of their way to use a mineral bath?"

"Well you never know, I was thinking it could be something more like those monkeys that lived in the hot springs—something like a quasi-tour—but then you can relax at the end. They could see the other rooms and learn history about the place too."

"Interesting," Anik said again. Something about the toast tasted better to him today.

"The problem is—besides the one, or ones, that you're thinking of—that presumably Dwaine disassembled the elevator that connects people to the cool rooms and it's in such a state that neither of us are going to be able to fix it," said Gwendoline. Anik's slight smile made her uneasy, as if he was preparing to shut her down.

"That certainly is a problem. The problem that I thought of—that you know that I thought of, that I already said—is that no one who lives here is going to go out there and no one is going to fly here just to use a mineral bath."

"I agree with you on some fronts, but I think this could be a good tourist attraction now that the coolest and most interesting parts are hypothetically accessible." The conversation was going almost exactly how Gwendoline predicted it would.

"So then how do you fix the elevator?" said Anik in a slightly condescending tone. He checked himself, reminding his brain that these young people were not in need of condescension—unlike most others in the community.

"Not sure. We were hoping that you would know someone who'd be able to fix, or potentially build a new one."

Anik couldn't suppress a sharp laugh. "I do know people, but doesn't that hole go miles down? I think you're going to have some issues getting that much cable."

"So, what I'm getting is that you don't know anywhere where we could get cables that long," said Gwendoline.

"I can't say that I do. I know multiple people who could do it, but I don't think that they're gonna want to."

"That's understandable." She smiled and scratched Louis's neck. Even expecting this outcome, she was disappointed, having tricked herself into thinking there could've been something she'd overlooked.

Anik continued, "I suppose that I can't stop you from making the Industrial Centre public, but I don't know if that's worth the burden that it would put on you two."

"I agree," said Nuru, taking the mayor's side for the

sake of poking holes in Gwendoline's dreams. Gwendoline side-eyed him and shook her head not more than an inch in either direction.

The mayor was now powered up and ready to use one of the few lines from which he still derived pleasure. He hadn't gotten to say it in at least three months, and, oh, what a turn of events! "Well, I'm sorry I couldn't have been more help." The two watched his ego reinflate as he took a large bite of toast, making sure to get a portion with a lot of peanut butter.

"I wasn't expecting you to be able to help much, truthfully," said Gwendoline. "I did, however, want to make sure that you knew that Dwaine had died and that the two of us are the new Dwaine."

He finished chewing before responding. "It's good to know. Having two original community residents being a part of it will ultimately be good for the community—a community built around the construction of that facility, but has been isolated from its goings-on." Anik was in full mayor mode doing the best part of his job from the comfort of his living room. What a life!

Gwendoline picked up on the banal political rhetoric and ignored it. She switched her attention to Louis and started dragging his paws toward her causing him to stir. Nuru, also not wanting to get hit with more canned mayoral responses, filled the break in conversation, "This is really good toast."

Anik nodded in agreement. His ego began to deflate as his mind shifted away from local politics back to the death of the one who had inadvertently contributed to the death of his love. "I have phases where I get this bread and then I have phases where I get the generic bread but I think I prefer the phases in which I have this bread."

"As far as phases go, I'd say that's a good phase to have," said Nuru, though he wondered what type of person would verbally announce that they have phases where they buy different types of bread.

"I have had worse phases than that, and I suppose I still *have* worse phases." At this point, Anik realized his statement may have constituted TMI and deferred speaking to someone else. Nuru glanced at Gwendoline to see her reaction but couldn't decipher her face.

"But you're doing alright now?" said Gwendoline, unfortunately proving to Nuru she wanted to dive deeper into Anik's inner thoughts.

"I'm doing alright now. I've done better and I've done worse. I'm doing about the same, living in the gray."

"The gray is a good spot to be in," said Gwendoline. "They always say that if there was no good there would be no bad, no happiness without sadness, no darkness without light, but no one ever thinks of the combination of the two."

"A homogeneous mixture . . ." said Anik. "Without the gray there is no black nor white." He took the last bite of his toast and wondered if his words made any sense. "I think about myself sometimes and I never come to any conclusions," he said, swallowing the last bit. He became immediately alarmed at the nonsense he'd spoken, but remembered that at least one of the two seemed to appreciate comments made in that vein.

"Sometimes I do that too, but I guess I never pose any questions," said Gwendoline. She wasn't sure if she actually did was Anik suggested, but she wanted to coax his train of thought down the tracks.

"Eh, I don't know what I'm getting at. I guess I'm just saying that for being alive so long I still don't understand my own motivations and my emotions."

"Seems like a pretty common thing. Maybe that's part of the whole being human thing."

Nuru sensed things would continue down a path of phrases uttered by people who are staring off into space and acted quickly to get the conversation back to something less abstract. "That toast was frickin' *really* good."

"You want another two slices?" asked Anik, happy to hear that Nuru liked the toast and more happy to use up his bread.

"I better not. I have my own food I should probably eat. This reminds me that I need to eat more peanut butter though."

Gwendoline looked at Nuru, taking a second to process what he'd said and she came to the realization that he wanted to leave.

"I don't think that I was even offered some!" she said. Thankfully, her thoughts hadn't gone deep enough into the world of quack theories to be mired there for the remainder of the day.

"Oh shoot, I thought I did but maybe I didn't. I'm sorry no matter what though," said Anik. A little color appeared in his cheeks.

"I would've declined the food anyway, don't worry about it."

"I'll try not to, but don't quote me on that."

"I won't, but if my life depends on it, I might."

"Well I suppose we should probably get going and leave you to eat," said Nuru as he got up. "I don't want to bother you and we also have our own things to worry about this afternoon."

"I believe it," said Anik, recovering the paleness in his face, "you have a lot of power at your disposal."

Nuru started putting on his outerwear and Gwendoline reluctantly joined him. "Yep," Nuru said, straining his voice, "gotta hose down the aircraft. Looks like whoever used it last ran it through the mud." Gwendoline looked at Nuru and half-frowned.

"Well I'm sorry to see you guys go so soon after arriving but I appreciate you passing along the intel."

"It was our pleasure and thanks for allowing my friend to eat your food," said Gwendoline. Louis was excited at this point and stood with his tail wagging as they escaped the building, Louis unfortunately not making it out with them.

"Good luck out there," said Anik. He was in a good mood now.

CHAPTER FIVE

After a quick pit stop to the FDC for peanut butter, they found their livingspace temperature had returned to normal.

"I'd say that went just about how I expected it would," said Gwendoline. She sat on the couch and looked out the window but was unable to see anything except her own reflection. Nuru didn't respond, he'd just had a stroke of culinary genius. "What do you think about all of it?"

"I think mixing peanut butter and avocado is gonna be the next big thing in my life," he said while starting to pit an avocado.

"I was kinda talking about the thing with the Industrial Centre," she squinted her eyes to see if she could focus on anything outside the window. "And yes, I know that you knew what I meant, and I clarified because I was playing along with the gag." Nuru didn't respond, the avocado was now sliced and ready to be mashed. "Whatever."

"Do you think that I should mix the peanut butter together with the avocado or do a layer of peanut butter and then a layer of avocado on the toast?"

"I don't know. I don't think I'd do either, really. Seems like the two flavors wouldn't complement each other."

"That's for me to not know and me to find out." He decided against mixing them together and opted for the two layer approach. "I don't think Dwaine intended us to do anything at that place. I bet he just used our names because he needed a name."

"Yeah, that's probably it."

"Do we try and get the elevator fixed? And by 'we' I mean you, but I'll help I guess." His toast was almost ready and he got out a plate.

"I think we probably should. Maybe go there and take an inventory of the elevator's parts. See how easy it is to get it all back up and running."

"Seems like we've got our work cut out for us."

"I suppose so. Maybe we rappel down to check everything out at first. The obligation's tug is becoming weaker though."

"Sounds like a lot of exercise." His toast popped and he dropped it on his plate.

"That it does." Gwendoline tried a third time at a slightly different angle to see out the window, but still all she saw was a distorted reflection of the livingspace. "I suppose we'll have to do something at some point."

"Eh, I guess maybe. I doubt Dwaine would've wanted us to bullshit around if we were doing our own things though."

"Yeah you're probably right. I just wonder what my own thing is then."

"I don't know, maybe, for example, the stuff you do." He finished spreading the toast and sat at his personal computer.

"I wonder what I'll think about this whole situation when I'm older. If it will become just a good story to tell or if it will inform my subconscious in some way that I won't understand."

"It might. It certainly could do both, if you haven't died of cancer already." He took a bite and his eyes sank.

Gwendoline smiled, allowing selfish vindication to poison her body. "I just wonder if I'll look back at how fucking dumb we—I—was even if I'm still as dumb then as I am now. Or maybe I'll look back and be impressed at how much energy we had for such adventures like breaking into a house. Hard to tell at this stage."

"I agree. I know I'll look back and realize that these two toppings—however good they are on their own—do not go together."

"Well, I coulda told you that, and did."

"True." With his mouth full he continued, "It's getting better though."

"I question my motivations for my activities sometimes and I wonder if in the future I'll look back from a higher or lower plane of existence with fondness of my former self or with regret, watching myself go from un-burned out to burned out."

"I don't know, there's still a good chance that both of us will die from radiation exposure before we're fifty so my bet is on us looking back with how stupid we were."

"I think that's a fair call, but what if we don't and we

live until our nineties and look back and say that we never accomplished anything or made anything."

"Eh, who gives a fuck about that?" he said, taking another bite of his toast, "For all we know we could look back and say all the time we spent trying to accomplish stuff was a waste. There doesn't seem to be any way of knowing how future us will judge the value of our own lives or actions."

"That's fair, but what if we're both old and still don't know how to summarize our lives?"

"I don't know, I'm sure we'll have amassed enough wisdom to do so. Anyway, we'll cross that bridge when we get to it."

"I suppose that's really all we can do." She stole a slice of Nuru's toast and bit into it. She caught herself in a facial expression that she realized conveyed more clearly and accurately her feelings than the sentence she was about to construct. "This isn't actually that terrible."

ACKNOWLEDGMENTS

Thanks to Taylor Sharp for being the first reader and providing spiritual and technical guidance throughout the entire writing process. Your insights gave me the power to type away while others loudly sang novelty songs one room over.

Thanks to Judy Gilats for tracking down errors ranging from subtle to flagrant and for making the text of this book nice and pretty. I appreciate the opportunities you've given me.

Thanks to William Bjorndal, Lee Bjorndal, and Adam Kranz for your criticism on early drafts of this book. I couldn't make you all happy, but I tried to.

Thanks to Josh Klein for looking this over and finding even more problems.

Thanks to my mother, Judy Bjorndal, for being supportive of all my good ideas and skeptical of all my bad ones.

Thanks to inspirational figures The Hussalonia Founder, Elliott Earls, Andrew W. K., and Eugene Tssui.

ABOUT THE AUTHOR

Peter Bjorndal is a multidisciplinary artist from Minnesota.